MIS

GOR

and the Mystery

TY
DON
of the Ghost Pirates

Kim Kennedy

Illustrations by Greg Call

AMULET BOOKS, NEW YORK

PUBLISHER'S NOTE: This is a work of fiction. Names, characters, places, and incidents are either the product of the author's imagination or are used fictitiously, and any resemblance to actual persons, living or dead, business establishments, events, or locales is entirely coincidental.

Library of Congress Cataloging-in-Publication Data:
Kennedy, Kim.
Misty Gordon / by Kim Kennedy.
p. cm.
Summary: While assisting her father, an estate and antiques dealer, teenaged Misty discovers a journal and pair of glasses that allow her to see ghosts, including those of pirates who founded her New England town and who are seeking a golden statue with mystical powers.
ISBN 978-0-8109-9357-0
[1. Ghosts—Fiction. 2. Pirates—Fiction. 3. Eyeglasses—Fiction. 4. Antiques—Fiction. 5. Family life—New England—Fiction. 6. New England—Fiction. 7. Mystery and detective stories.] I. Title.

PZ7.K3843Mis 2010
[Fic]—dc22
2009011248

Text copyright © 2010 Kim Kennedy
Illustrations copyright © 2010 Greg Call
Book design by Melissa Arnst

Printed and bound in U.S.A.
10 9 8 7 6 5 4 3 2 1

Amulet Books are available at special discounts when purchased in quantity for premiums and promotions as well as fundraising or educational use. Special editions can also be created to specification. For details, contact specialmarkets@abramsbooks.com or the address below.

ABRAMS
THE ART OF BOOKS SINCE 1949
115 West 18th Street
New York, NY 10011
www.abramsbooks.com

09 10

- To my brother Glenn Kennedy -

Contents

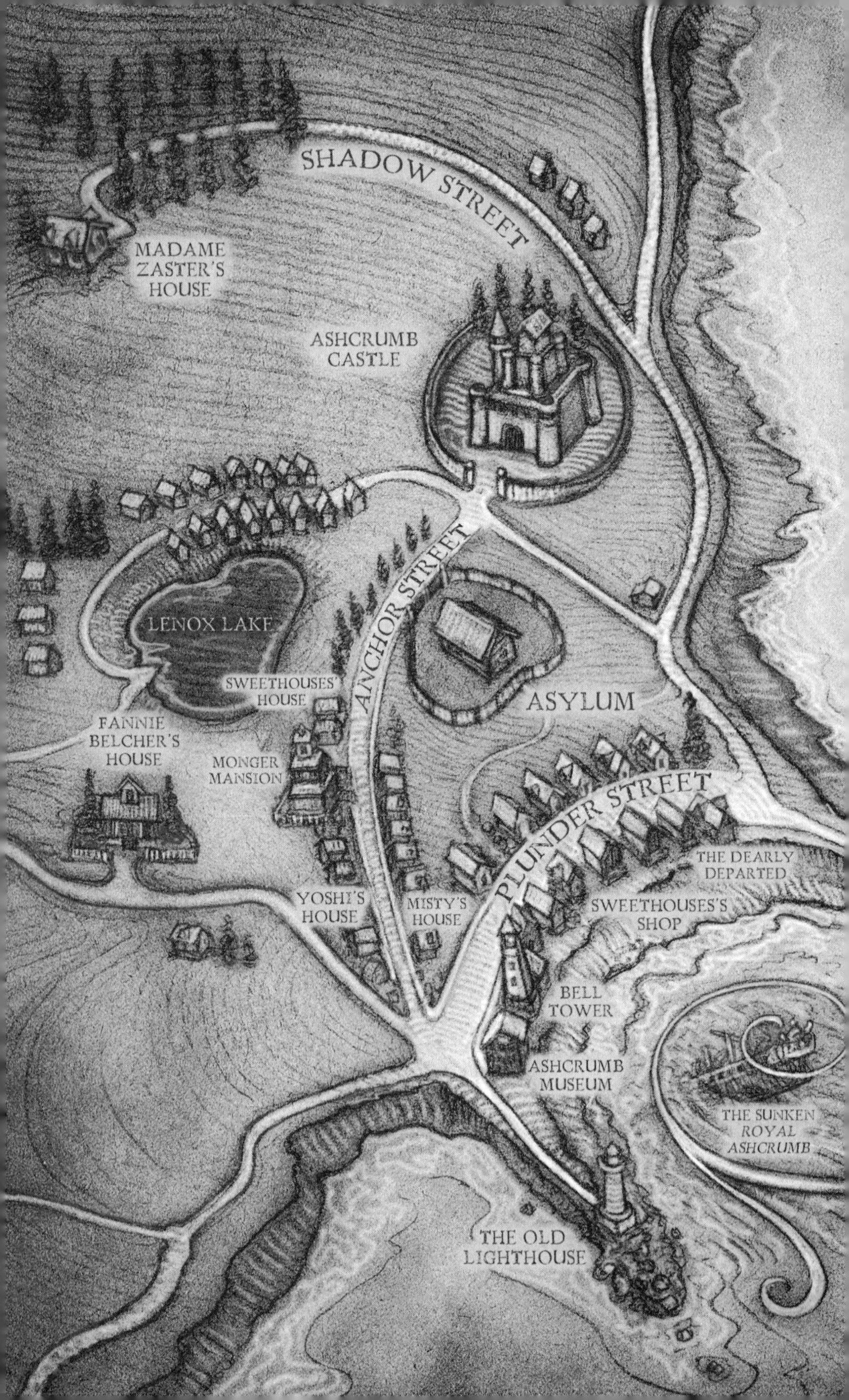
SHADOW STREET
MADAME ZASTER'S HOUSE
ASHCRUMB CASTLE
LENOX LAKE
ANCHOR STREET
SWEETHOUSES' HOUSE
ASYLUM
FANNIE BELCHER'S HOUSE
MONGER MANSION
PLUNDER STREET
THE DEARLY DEPARTED
YOSHI'S HOUSE
MISTY'S HOUSE
SWEETHOUSES'S SHOP
BELL TOWER
ASHCRUMB MUSEUM
THE SUNKEN *ROYAL ASHCRUMB*
THE OLD LIGHTHOUSE

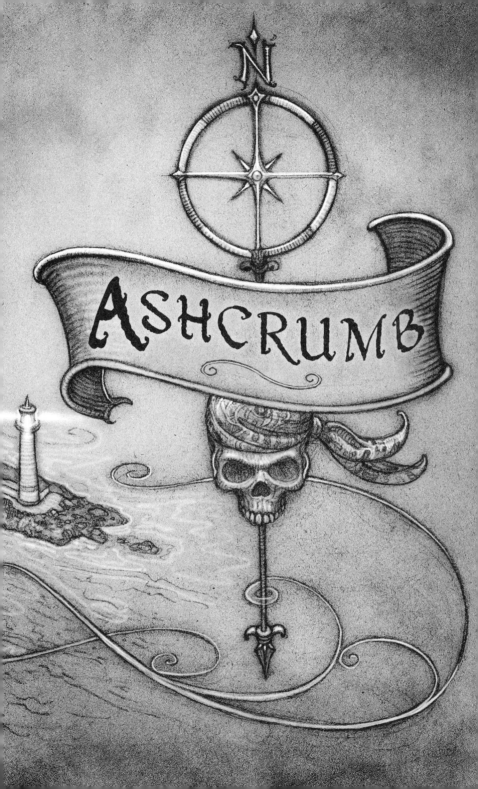

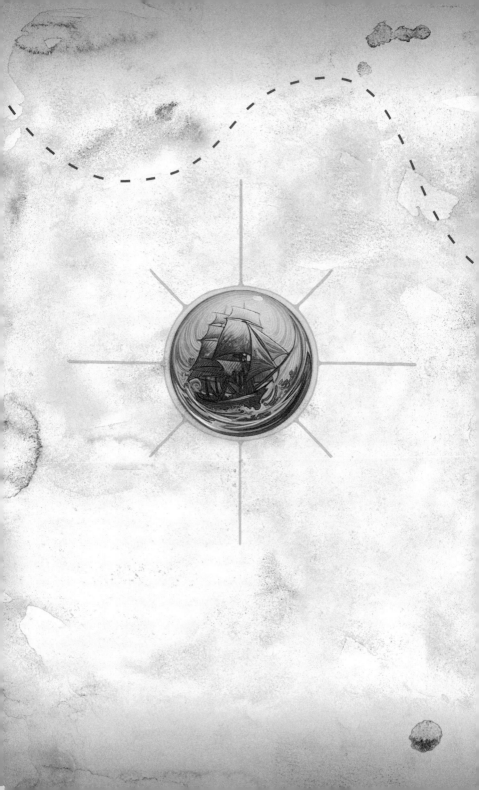

MISTY GORDON

and the Mystery of the Ghost Pirates -

1

Fannie Belcher's Things

Mr. and Mrs. Gordon liked it when people died. Not that they were bizarre or unfeeling, it's just that the Gordons' business depended on death. You see, they owned the Dearly Departed Antiques Store, a shop filled with the musty old furniture of the recently deceased.

Perhaps it was a bit gloomy and creepy, the way the Gordons made their living, but they didn't mind. Rather, they fancied themselves the best in the business. And the fastest. As soon as someone "bit the dust," the Gordons would purchase his or her stuff. Their motto? *We buy the bucket as soon as you kick it.*

In fact, to learn of a death in the historic little sea town of

Ashcrumb, one only had to spy the Gordons' company truck traveling down the street. Faded green, with D.E.A.D. painted on its side, the former ice-cream truck—which still played its music—was quite the town spectacle. Curious kids on bikes would follow the truck, all the while guessing where it might stop. *Who died?* they would wonder. *Was it Mr. Fulton, the cat-hater? Or was it Hazel Monger, the freaky hermit?*

One Saturday morning in October, blaring its warped tunes, the truck attracted its largest group ever. Twenty kids trailed behind it, pedaling down shady streets, through sleepy neighborhoods, and past ancient cemeteries. Finally, the truck came to a sputtering stop in front of a weathered mansion.

The huge place had been the home of Fannie Belcher, the richest old lady in Ashcrumb. And lucky Mr. Gordon was the first in line to pick over her belongings. He could barely contain his excitement as he hopped out of his truck.

He nodded at the group of sweaty, panting kids, all of them waiting to see who would answer the late Fannie Belcher's door. Maybe, they hoped, it would be the ghost of Fannie Belcher herself.

"Hurry up and ring the doorbell!" yelled Hector Figg, a freckle-faced boy. He swayed impatiently atop his banana seat. "We don't have all day!"

"Shhh," said Mr. Gordon, smoothing his shirt over his round

belly. "Hector, you kids go on home. This isn't a sideshow. Have a little respect."

Mr. Gordon grabbed the mammoth door knocker. After a few clanks, the door creaked open, revealing a long-faced man in a black uniform.

"Yes?" wheezed the butler, glaring at Mr. Gordon. "Who are you?"

"I'm your DEAD!" said Mr. Gordon brightly.

The butler danced backward, a look of horror on his face. "*Dead?*"

"That's right," said Mr. Gordon, sticking his foot inside the doorway. "It stands for Deceased's Estate and Antiques Dealer. I'm Frank Gordon. I'm here to purchase Ms. Belcher's things."

"Oh, of course," said the butler. "Come in."

Mr. Gordon bolted inside and slammed the door.

The kids rushed to the windows and peered through the broken shutters. They snickered, watching Mr. Gordon's bulky figure lurch about the dreary place, picking up chairs, examining sofas, and rummaging through drawers.

"He looks like a big rat," said Hector.

"Yeah," added another kid, smacking gum. "A rat that just found the biggest hunk of cheese in the world."

That evening, his truck crammed with Fannie Belcher's stuff, Mr. Gordon squeezed himself behind the steering wheel and began his drive home. He had really scored this time! He couldn't wait to see the look on his wife's face when she saw what he'd bought.

Humming along to the ice-cream truck's music, Mr. Gordon turned onto cobblestoned Anchor Street. He smiled broadly as he pulled in front of his little white house nestled among crimson maple trees.

"I'm back!" he announced, bounding into his house, where Mrs. Gordon sat, painting her toenails.

Mr. Gordon held up a lumpy sack. "Guess what I've got in here."

"What?" squealed Mrs. Gordon. "Is it something from rich old Fannie Belcher's house?"

"Right you are," bellowed Mr. Gordon, pulling out what looked like a dead animal. He tossed it to his wife.

"A mink coat!" she gasped, putting it on.

"Belcher never went anywhere without it!" said Mr. Gordon.

"And I can see why!" said Mrs. Gordon, elated. "Oh, what luxury!" she purred, modeling the coat. "Such marvelous cuffs and deep pockets!"

Around the couch she twirled in the coat, dropping nasty tufts of fur on the floor.

Shielding his face from the flying fur was James, the Gordons' eight-year-old son.

"Gross," James gagged. "That thing is shedding."

"Expensive furs are like that," coughed Mr. Gordon. "They have to get used to their new owners."

"That's right," agreed Mrs. Gordon, burying her plump face in the musky mink.

"James," said Mr. Gordon, digging around in the bag, "I've got something for you, too!"

He handed James a real stuffed squirrel.

"Cool!" said James, staring in amazement at the rodent. Its face was frozen in a strange smile, its two yellow teeth sticking out from crinkled whiskers.

While James stroked his petrified friend and Mrs. Gordon tripped about in her molting coat, Mr. Gordon began feeling around in his bag again.

Observing all of this in total shock and embarrassment was Misty Gordon. She sat dumbfounded on the couch, sinking lower and lower into its cushions. She couldn't help thinking how much her dad looked like a scatterbrained Santa Claus, handing out gifts from a sack he'd lost one hundred years ago and just found again.

Misty had watched this same drama unfold over and over throughout her entire life, but still, even after eleven years, she'd never grown accustomed to it. Wondering what her dad might pull out of that bag always filled her with dread.

"Last but not least," said Mr. Gordon, pausing dramatically with his hand in the bag. "I've got something for Misty!"

Misty cringed.

"You know how you've been begging for your own phone?" he said. "Well, feast your eyes on this!"

With that, he pulled out a heavy, black phone from the 1940s and handed it to Misty.

"Your very first phone," said Mr. Gordon, beaming. "And with a little luck, maybe I can get the thing to work."

"Great," moaned Misty, looking at the phone's frayed cord. "So I got a dead lady's broken phone."

"What a dud!" chuckled James. "But they can't all be winners. Isn't that right, Dad?"

Misty grabbed the phone, shoved James out of the way, and went upstairs to her room, shutting her door. She looked around and sighed. Everything she had was antique. Her rickety four-poster bed leaned in the corner with a faded patchwork quilt atop it and Misty's book satchel—an old leather mailbag—hanging from one of its posts. Yellowed lace curtains fluttered in the open window, under which her desk stood, looking like something George Washington might have used. As a boy.

"Another item for the Misty Museum," she said sarcastically, setting the phone on her desk. Too bad the phone didn't work.

She would have called her best friend, Yoshiko, and told her all about the latest craziness in the Gordon household. After all, if there was anybody who understood craziness, it was Yoshi, as everyone called her. Her dad was Dr. Yamamoto, the famous psychiatrist who ran Ashcrumb's insane asylum.

A chill wind passed through the room, and Misty shivered. She pushed the window shut and then opened her closet and grabbed a fuzzy wool sweater, one of the many that her dad had given her. It was ugly, but at least it was warm. She tried to wrestle it on, but the thing had become so speckled with holes that she couldn't figure out which one was for her head.

"Forget it!" she said, exasperated. With a crackle of static, Misty yanked off the sweater, sending her brown hair flying out in all directions. She straightened her glasses, disgusted. A few vintage clothes were cool, but an entire wardrobe of the stuff? What she wouldn't give for something new. But that required money. *I'm just gonna have to do more babysitting,* she decided, putting the sweater back.

Just then, a loud clang sounded behind Misty, causing her to jump. She whirled around—expecting to see James with one of his obnoxious, noisy toys—only to find no one there.

Misty glanced about. "Ha-ha . . . *very* funny, James," she said, crossing her arms. "I know you're hiding in here."

An even louder clang sounded, followed by a strange rustle.

Misty squinted suspiciously at the dark space beneath her bed. In a flash, she tossed the bed skirt aside and looked beneath the saggy mattress. A couple of old dolls peered back from the gloom, but not James.

A string of dull thumps erupted, sending Misty's head shooting back out from under the bed.

"What *is* that?" she said, irritated. Then Misty's eyes fell upon Fannie Belcher's telephone, and her mouth dropped open.

"No way," she whispered in astonishment as she realized that the noises were coming from the broken phone—noises that sounded more like beatings than rings. *Noises that sounded as if something inside the phone were trying to get out.*

Misty ventured shakily toward the phone and picked it up to have a look. Suddenly, the phone jerked in her hands, and its underside panel popped loose. Out from it dropped something small and dark.

Misty yelped as the object landed on her desk and skittered toward the window. In a blur, it flew at the windowpane, hitting the glass with a terrible *SMACK*! It flapped wildly for a moment and then fluttered miserably to the floor.

For a brief moment, Misty thought the motionless clump

was a bird that had somehow gotten trapped in the phone. But when Misty crouched over it, she gasped to discover that it wasn't a bird at all. It was a *book*.

"What the—" said Misty, gazing dumbstruck at the slender, black journal. Chills running down her spine, Misty read the embossed letters on its cover: DIARY OF FANNIE BELCHER.

There was a knock on her door.

"Just a minute!" said Misty, snatching up the diary. She tossed the slim book into one of her desk drawers and slammed it shut. Like a caged animal, the diary immediately started banging against the compartment.

"Misty?" her father called outside her door.

Just like that, the diary went quiet. Misty blinked, puzzled.

"Yes," Misty called back, plopping on her bed and trying to look composed. "Come in."

The door opened, and her father stuck his head in. "Is everything all right?" he asked. "I heard a lot of noise coming from your room."

"Noise?" said Misty, thinking quickly. "Oh—er—I accidentally dropped the phone, that's all."

"Oh, I see," said Mr. Gordon, glancing at the phone, which lay dismantled atop Misty's desk. He walked over and picked it up. "Panel came loose," he mumbled, tinkering with it. "Lemme see if this'll work . . . just give me a second . . . this thing is made out of steel, ya know . . . they don't make stuff like this anymore."

While he messed with the phone, Misty kept a nervous—and curious—eye on the desk drawer. Why had the diary gone silent when her father entered the room?

"There you go," Mr. Gordon said, finally getting the panel back in place and setting the phone down. "Anyway, dinner is ready."

"Oh, okay," said Misty, still staring at the drawer as her father turned to leave. "I'll be down in a minute."

The very moment Mr. Gordon shut the door—*WHUMP!* went the diary.

What is going on here? thought Misty. Not only did she have a crazy diary on her hands, she had one that was obviously avoiding her father. As bewildered—and frightened—as Misty felt, she couldn't help but grin. It looked like her days of getting "duds" were over!

Misty didn't get much sleep that night. Around midnight, the diary started knocking against the drawer with a relentless clunk-clunk-clunk. Then, around two o'clock, an awful shuffling noise came from the hallway. Misty sat up in bed and listened. Was it an animal? Had a window been left open? Misty didn't want to find out. Finally, at four in the morning, the diary quit banging around, and Misty managed to doze off. But not for long.

She woke to the sounds of her mother making breakfast. Between the clatter of dishes and the crash of a skillet, Misty rolled over in bed and tried to go back to sleep, but it was too late. James had obviously awakened, judging by the racket coming from his room—quick footsteps to the bathroom and the flush of a toilet. Misty braced herself as the house's tired pipes clanked and vibrated, sending a light snow of ceiling plaster onto her bed.

You could hear everything in their house, which made Misty wonder if she had been the only one who'd heard the strange, shuffling noise coming from the hallway last night. And there were no sounds from the desk. Maybe she had dreamed it all.

"Breakfast is ready!" her mother called.

Misty and James plodded sleepily down the stairs. They met their father at the bottom, just as he was emerging from his study.

"Good morning," Mr. Gordon said, locking the study door behind him.

Misty and James grunted a groggy reply.

The kitchen was filled with smoke, Mrs. Gordon having burned the toast again. Not that her husband noticed. He crunched happily on the blackened bread as he read the newspaper. By the cheery look on his face, Misty could tell that he'd just read the obituaries.

"Kids, you won't believe who died," he said. "It's simply marvelous!"

"It's otherworldly," giggled their mother.

"What do you mean, *otherworldly*?" asked James.

"Well," said Mr. Gordon, attacking some bacon. "Madame Zaster has died, or as one of her kind might say, 'Madame Zaster has passed into another dimension.'" He mused, a fleck of grease shining on his chin.

"You mean Madame Zaster the town psychic?" asked Misty.

"Yes," said Mr. Gordon. "She was quite a fortune-teller and hypnotist. She'd been reading palms and holding séances for years. You know," he added, his fork in the air, "she was also a clairvoyant."

"What's that?" asked James.

"A clairvoyant is somebody who can see into another realm, the realm of spirits and ghosts and the past and future," Mr. Gordon rattled on, polishing off the rest of his breakfast.

"Creepy," said James. "Are you gonna get her stuff? I bet she had some freaky things."

"As a matter of fact, I'm on my way to her place right now," Mr. Gordon announced, standing up and collecting his papers. "I'm sure I'll find some strange things, but nothing fancy. Madame Zaster wasn't the type to own mink coats."

"Speaking of coats," said Mrs. Gordon, a curious look on her face. "It's the oddest thing! I hung Fannie Belcher's mink coat in the closet upstairs last night, and this morning it's gone. It's as if it just walked out of here on its own!"

Misty gulped.

"Are you sure you didn't put it in the box for the store by mistake?" asked Mr. Gordon. "I'll check when I get back. But now I'd better be on my way. Mrs. Neck, the realtor, is going to meet me at Madame Zaster's house, and I don't want to be late. You kids want to come along?"

James shook his head. "Hector is coming over. We're gonna be doing kung fu."

"How about you, Misty?" said Mr. Gordon. "Want to ride to Madame Zaster's with me?"

"No thanks," Misty said. "Not after what happened the last time I rode in the company truck."

"Dear, you're going to have to forget about all *that*," said Mrs. Gordon, patting Misty's hand.

"That's easy for you to say," said Misty, flipping her hair behind her shoulders. "How would you like it if you were riding in that truck and people on the street started pointing and laughing and calling you a vulture?"

"Sweetheart, we've gone over this a thousand times," said Mrs. Gordon. "We're not vultures. We're *estate brokers*."

Misty rolled her eyes.

"So you're not going?" said Mrs. Gordon. "Good! Then you can watch James and Hector in the yard while I get some things done indoors."

The thought of watching her brother and his smelly best friend do sloppy kung fu moves on the front lawn was more than Misty could bear.

"I've changed my mind," Misty said quickly to her dad. "I'm going with you to Madame Zaster's."

"Well then, let's hit the road," said Mr. Gordon.

"Take your satchel with you," Mrs. Gordon told Misty. "You might see something at Madame Zaster's house that you'd like to keep."

With her old mailbag slung over her shoulder, Misty climbed into the company truck with her dad. After a few false starts, the vehicle chugged alive, sending its ice-cream music into the air.

"Dad," said Misty, "why don't you disconnect that music?"

"This truck is an antique," he explained, turning onto the street. "By playing its music, I am respecting its history."

Misty sighed. She knew the real reason the truck still played the music was because her dad couldn't figure out how to disconnect its speaker wires.

They'd only been driving a moment, and already the truck was attracting its usual crowd of bicyclers.

"The morbid-curiosity posse is up early this morning," noted Mr. Gordon, looking in his side-view mirror.

Misty looked out the window as they passed foggy Ashcrumb Bay, where nearly four hundred years ago the *Royal Ashcrumb*—the English ship for which the town was named—had sunk. Through the breaks in the fog, Misty could see some people walking their dogs along the beach.

"Looks like the new lighthouse is coming along nicely," said Mr. Gordon, pointing to a construction site on a piece of rock jutting into the sea. But Misty wasn't paying attention. She was busy checking out the pumpkin patch on the other side of the street, where the tops of the orange globes peeked out from the mist.

On they drove to the edge of town, where white picket fences were scarce and crumbling houses were plenty. This was the creepiest part of Ashcrumb.

They turned onto Shadow Street. One of the oldest streets in town, the narrow road was lined on both sides with ancient elm trees. Misty sank into her seat as the knobby limbs scraped the roof of the truck like fingernails across a chalkboard.

Mr. Gordon checked the side-view mirror. The children on

bikes had disappeared. Obviously, they hadn't liked the look of things.

"I haven't been down this street since I was a boy," Mr. Gordon recalled with a shiver. "We used to call it the tree tunnel."

"And what's at the end of this . . . tree tunnel?" asked Misty.

"Madame Zaster's house," he replied.

Just when Misty thought the trees couldn't get any thicker and lower, she and her dad arrived at the end of the street, where a little house stood. It reminded Misty of the witch's cottage in the Hänsel and Gretel story. Except there were definitely no lollipops around this place.

"It hasn't changed a bit," said Mr. Gordon, stopping the truck. "And if I remember correctly, there were lots of cats around here."

At that moment, a large tabby sprang onto the windshield. Mr. Gordon jumped, accidentally hitting the horn. It was a clown horn, and the obnoxious *WHAH-WHAH* sent the cat three feet into the air and onto the ground. It hissed and skittered into some wild rose bushes.

"Sorry," said Mr. Gordon sheepishly.

They got out of the truck and had a look around. The yard was completely overgrown with grass and vines, except for a narrow path made of shells and small stepping-stones leading to the front door. Mr. Gordon and Misty had just started to follow the path when they heard something rustle behind them.

They each gave a yelp and stood stock-still until a voice called out, "Yoo-hoo! Frank Gordon, is that you?"

It was Mrs. Neck, the realtor. She looked as relieved to see them as they were to see her. She plowed through the tall weeds and shook Mr. Gordon's hand.

"Are you going to be selling Madame Zaster's house?" Misty asked Mrs. Neck as they all ambled to the house.

"Well, I'm going to *try* to sell it," said Mrs. Neck. "But frankly, I don't know who in their right mind would buy this place. It's in terrible shape." She dug around in her purse and pulled out a key. "Anyway, Madame Zaster's children didn't want any of the furnishings, so you can pick what you like."

This is exactly what Mr. Gordon wanted to hear. He gingerly took the key from Mrs. Neck's hand and unlocked the door.

If the outside of the house looked untamed, it was nothing compared to the way the inside looked. Vines had crept through the windows, the dark green tendrils snaking along the cracked ceiling. Furniture stood covered in dust and cobwebs, and here and there a cat slept, the felines having wandered in through one of the many holes in the walls.

"Good grief," said Misty. "This place is a mess. How could Madame Zaster have lived here?"

"Oh, she hadn't lived here for years," said Mrs. Neck, fanning away a spider. "She became ill and so had been living with her children when she died." Another spider came drifting toward Mrs. Neck. "Well, if you need me, I'll be outside waiting for my associate to arrive." Then she stumbled back out the front door.

No sooner had Mrs. Neck left than Mr. Gordon called from the next room, "Look what I found!"

Misty stepped inside the dim parlor, where her father was hopping up and down next to a round table, around which sat five chairs. In the middle of the table was a crystal ball.

"It's Madame Zaster's séance table!" Mr. Gordon sang. He nodded his head and hummed, a sign that he'd found something rare—and valuable.

"Do you know what this means?" he beamed, waving his arms over the table and chairs like a game show host. "This is a complete set. Talk about fetching a pretty penny!"

He picked up the dust-laden crystal ball, studied it for a second, then put it back down. "This hunk of glass is probably worthless, though. It might make a good paperweight," he snorted, giving Misty a nudge with his elbow.

At that moment, a chandelier above the table started to

sway. As it creaked back and forth, a hollow sound passed through the house. The lights in the chandelier blazed on, flickered, and then went dead.

"What was that?" said Misty, grabbing hold of her dad.

"Probably nothing," Mr. Gordon said, shrugging his shoulders. "It's an old house. They're filled with strange noises and electrical problems and—Whoa! I don't believe my eyes!" Mr. Gordon shouted in glee, bounding toward a stained-glass floor lamp. "This looks like a Tiffany lamp! Boy, oh boy, oh boy!"

While Mr. Gordon drooled over the lamp, Misty hesitantly ventured around the house. She made her way down the narrow hall and into a little room. It was empty, except for a vanity. It was a dainty piece of wooden furniture, with an oval mirror and drawers. Misty glided her hand atop its cool surface, then opened one of the drawers.

"What's this?" she said, surprised to find that the compartment contained a few things. Among the odds and ends were a slender box and pair of cat-eye glasses. Misty took out the box and read its top: THE HYPNO-CLOCK.

Misty removed the box's lid. Inside it was a strange-looking old pocket watch on a golden chain. As she touched it, the timepiece began ticking. She flipped it over and read the curious engraving upon its back:

Listen to the tick and listen to the tock,
You're growing ever-sleepy to the swinging Hypno-Clock.

Madame Zaster must have used this for hypnotizing people, thought Misty, putting the watch back into its box. Then she took the cat-eye glasses from the drawer. Just for fun, she took off her own glasses and slipped on Madame Zaster's.

Usually, when she traded glasses with kids at school, she could never see clearly through their lenses. But to Misty's amazement, she could see perfectly through these glasses.

"How weird!" she laughed aloud. Then she jumped, startled to see a tall woman standing in the doorway. The lady was wearing a dark purple dress and old-fashioned shoes. Her black hair hung in thick curls about her face, and she didn't look happy.

"I'm sorry," said Misty, guessing the woman was Mrs. Neck's associate. "I probably shouldn't be going through these things. I just wanted to see—"

"*You will* see *much*," said the woman, with a piercing stare.

The stranger's voice sounded like it had static, as if it were coming from a radio.

"Excuse me?" said Misty.

The woman pointed a finger at Misty and chanted, "*All will be revealed once you have learned the nature of the Golden Three . . . but first you must prove* your *nature to* me."

"I'm sorry," said Misty. "I don't understand."

Quickly, Misty took off the cat-eye glasses and put her own glasses back on. When she looked up, the woman was gone.

"What was *that* all about?" Misty whispered. "Mrs. Neck has one creepy associate! Oh well, *whatever*." She dropped the cat-eye glasses and Hypno-Clock into her satchel and then headed off to see what her dad was up to.

She found him outside, loading furniture into the truck while Mrs. Neck stood at the end of the driveway, checking her watch and tapping her foot.

"Whew!" Mr. Gordon gasped, dabbing his reddened face with a handkerchief. He turned to Misty. "I'm all done here. Did you find anything you liked?"

"Actually, I did find something," said Misty. "It's Madame Zaster's old vanity. Do you think there's enough room left in the truck for it?"

"I don't see why not," he replied.

Miraculously, Mr. Gordon managed to fit the vanity into the overstuffed truck. Finding a place for Misty to sit was another matter. She ended up sitting in the very back of the vehicle, perched atop the séance table.

The truck cranked on with its usual ice-cream music. A few cats tore out of the bushes as the truck started its way back down the weedy driveway.

Mr. Gordon stopped next to Mrs. Neck. "Thanks for everything," he called out the window.

"You're welcome," she said. "I'm sorry my associate never showed up. I know you could have used his help loading the furniture."

"No big deal," said Mr. Gordon. "Well, have a good afternoon." And away the truck chugged.

Misty blinked, pushing her glasses up the bridge of her nose.

"Did Mrs. Neck just say that her associate never showed up?" she called, trying to make her voice heard over the music.

"Yep," said Mr. Gordon.

"Then who was that woman in Madame Zaster's house?"

"*What* woman?" said Mr. Gordon.

"The woman with the curly black hair," said Misty. "She was wearing a purple dress."

Misty saw her father's eyes narrow in the rearview mirror.

"Surely you saw her!" said Misty, exasperated.

"No," he said, shifting gears. "I didn't."

Misty was completely baffled. Who had the mysterious woman been? She shuddered as she remembered the woman's chilling voice and her strange message.

Misty looked around her. The vanity was just in reach. She began to explore the other drawers. Opening one, she pulled out an old black-and-white photograph.

Her hand began to shake as she looked at the picture, for its image was none other than that of the woman she had met in the house. Misty flipped the picture over. Scribbled in ink was the signature:

Madame Zaster

"I think it's going to be quite an autumn," said Mr. Gordon cheerily as they passed the pumpkin patch.

"You can say that again," said Misty, dropping the photo into her bag.

2

The Ashcrumb Castle

Misty had never seen a storm gather so quickly. Within minutes, the skies had gone from a calm blue to a stormy gray.

"Look at the size of that cloud!" said Mr. Gordon, pointing out the window of the truck. "I'm afraid we're going to be driving right into it."

Misty looked. It was an eerie, dark green thundercloud, billowing menacingly over their neighborhood. Little threads of lightning streaked within it, illuminating its insides like a hazy fishbowl.

They pulled in front of their house just when the first drops of rain began to fall. James and his best friend, Hector

Figg, were on the front lawn, doing kung fu in weird black helmets.

"What are you boys doing out in this kind of weather?" Mr. Gordon bellowed as he spilled out of the truck. "You could get struck by lightning, you know!"

"Not while we're wearing our anti-lightning helmets," said Hector, rapping on the one atop his head. "They protect the skull up to a billion volts of electricity! They're my dad's invention."

"I see," said Mr. Gordon, impressed.

Hector's dad, Dr. Figg, was a mad scientist of sorts who, besides being a brilliant inventor, was in charge of the construction of Ashcrumb's new, high-tech lighthouse.

"So, was I right?" said James to his dad. "Did you find a lot of creepy stuff today?"

"Why creepy?" asked Hector, peeking into the truck. "Where did you go?"

"We went to Madame Zaster's house," replied Misty.

Just then, a bright green streak of lightning bolted from the sky, followed by an earsplitting thunderclap.

"Boys," said Mr. Gordon, opening the back of the truck. "Give me a hand with Madame Zaster's vanity. I want to get it inside before the storm hits."

The boys groaned.

"Don't worry," said Mr. Gordon. "It's the only piece of furniture we're unloading. I'm taking the rest of the stuff to the Dearly Departed."

They'd just moved the vanity into Misty's room when another thunderclap boomed. The rain began falling in sheets. It was a terrible storm, with blinding lightning and a howling wind that seemed bent on blowing the house down. Misty sat on the couch and stared out the window at the raging tempest.

This was the type of weather, Misty mused, that tossed ships at sea, sending them crashing onto the shore. The powerful lightning that was streaking outside was probably the same sort of wicked jolts that had struck the mast of the *Royal Ashcrumb*, sending the legendary vessel blazing and sinking to its watery grave in the town's bay.

A loud crack of thunder shook Misty from her thoughts. She put her hand in her bag and felt the thick paper of the photograph. She pulled it out and gazed at the dim image of Madame Zaster. Studying the woman's curling mouth and dark eyes, Misty knew without a doubt that she had met Madame Zaster's ghost. But why had she appeared to Misty?

It was still raining the next morning when Yoshi, who lived across the street, met Misty outside for their walk to school. Standing under a giant green umbrella, Yoshi looked even smaller than usual. Her long black hair was swirling in the wind as she clutched the handle of the umbrella.

"Should we wait for James?" asked Yoshi as Misty darted under the huge green dome.

"He already ran to school with Hector," said Misty.

A gust of wind blew at their backs as they started their wet walk, huddling like two ants carrying a leaf.

"I didn't think you and your family were getting back from your trip until tomorrow," said Misty.

"We had to cut our trip short," said Yoshi. "Dad had to get back to the asylum. There was an emergency."

"What do you mean?" said Misty.

"Well, I really shouldn't say," said Yoshi. "You know how I'm not supposed to talk about what goes on in the asylum. It's confidential."

"Tell me!" cried Misty. "I promise I won't say anything to anybody! Besides, I've got a secret to tell you, too. You go first."

"Okay," blurted Yoshi. "Here's the deal. There's this new patient at the asylum called May Nays. He's a major lunatic. He will do anything to get his hands on mayonnaise. I mean, he'll kill for the stuff. *Literally.*"

"He'll *kill* for mayonnaise?" snickered Misty. "Are you kidding?"

"No, I'm not kidding," said Yoshi. "Anyway, you know how werewolves go on a rampage during a full moon? Well, that's kinda how it is with May Nays. Except it isn't a full moon that makes May Nays crazy, it's stormy weather. And last night, when the storm hit, May Nays went berserk and busted out of his room. Thankfully, he didn't get far. They found him in the asylum's kitchen pantry, gorging himself on mayonnaise."

"That is completely twisted," said Misty.

"Tell me about it," agreed Yoshi. "So, now it's your turn. Tell me your secret."

There was so much that Misty wanted to tell Yoshi that she didn't know where to begin.

For a few seconds, Misty said nothing and just scurried along with her head down, watching autumn leaves float past on the flooded path while she thought of what to say.

Suddenly, they were met with the piercing screech of a whistle.

It was Margie Medford, the school's crossing guard. She was a large, horsey woman with bushy brows and a booming voice. She was also a menacing bully who loved to push kids around when parents and teachers weren't watching.

"Move it, move it, move it!" Medford shouted, waving Misty and Yoshi across the street. A small boy running with an armload of books slipped and fell down. Medford banged him on the head with her STOP sign. "Get up, Jimmy Winn, you little slowpoke!" she yelled, yanking him up by his ear and dragging him the rest of the way. She gave Misty and Yoshi a dark look as the girls dashed into the safety of the school's entrance.

Though, truth be told, Ashcrumb Elementary looked anything but safe. It looked downright scary. Originally built by King Charles I of England in 1633—when the town was a royal colony—Ashcrumb Elementary happened to be a *real* castle. It was gigantic, several stories tall, with vine-covered turrets stretching into the sky. A stone wall enclosed the castle's sprawling grounds that were filled with towering elm and maple trees, all of which had a nasty habit of scratching their limbs against the milky windowpanes of the school during class. In the far corners of the grounds stood little slate-roofed buildings. Once used for housing horses and carriages, the buildings now sheltered the teachers' cars.

The castle had everything a castle would have, except for a moat. Which was a bit of a shame, Misty always thought, because Margie Medford, who was quite the troll, would surely have relished hiding under a drawbridge.

At the moment, the crossing guard was stomping through a puddle to her next victims, a frightened group of first graders.

"I can't stand Medford," said Yoshi, collapsing her umbrella and shaking the raindrops from it. "My dad says she has issues with power and anger."

"What does *that* mean?" asked Misty.

"It means that she likes to terrorize small things because it makes her feel bigger," explained Yoshi.

"Oh," said Misty. "I guess your dad would know."

Yoshi's father, Dr. Yamamoto, was an expert at figuring people out. That's why he ran Ashcrumb's insane asylum. Yoshi had inherited her father's knack for understanding people. Not only was Yoshi the smartest person in the class, she was the most feared. Nobody dared mess with a girl whose father could lock you up and throw away the key.

Misty, on the other hand, was a different story altogether. She was smart, but she daydreamed a lot, gazing out the window instead of minding the chalkboard. Sometimes when teachers called on Misty, she didn't reply. It wasn't because she didn't know the answer, it was simply because her mind was a thousand miles away. While the other kids at school didn't bother Yoshi, they thrived on making Misty miserable. Her secondhand clothes, lopsided glasses, and family's odd business—not to mention the ice-cream truck—made her the target of endless jokes.

There was one girl in particular who loved to torture Misty. Her name was Alexis Lenox, a snobby, spoiled redhead. Not a day passed that Alexis didn't say something cruel to Misty.

Walking into the school, Misty winced to see Alexis and her crowd approaching.

"*Nice* coat," Alexis smirked, tugging on Misty's shabby trench coat. "I think I just saw some moths fly out of it!" Then Alexis gave a taunting pull on Misty's bag and sneered. "And just *what* is with this relic? Are you delivering mail for the Pony Express these days?"

Alexis let out a peal of laughter, and she and her friends sauntered off.

Misty's face reddened as she felt the familiar sting of embarrassment.

"Forget her," said Yoshi. "Alexis Lenox has issues with superiority. Anyway, what's your secret?"

Just then, over the intercom system came the voice of the school's principal, Mr. Ableman. "ALL STUDENTS REPORT TO TOWN FATHERS HALL FOR ASSEMBLY."

"I'll tell you after school," said Misty, completely deflated.

Town Fathers Hall was a cavernous, drafty chamber, with narrow and murky windows reaching to its vaulted ceiling.

Standing on the hall's dim stage, watching the students file into the building, were Principal Ableman and Vice Principal Barrel. While the short, bald Mr. Ableman tested the microphone, the tall, beady-eyed Mr. Barrel tilted his head back, as if watching the children through his nostrils. Plagued with bad nerves, Mr. Barrel had a twitchy eye. And in his back pocket he always kept a small paddle.

"Okay, okay, okay," said Mr. Ableman to the assemblage. "Everybody get to your seats."

"To your seats, to your seats," said Mr. Barrel.

Misty sat with the rest of her class, taking a seat next to the window. From her spot, she could see out onto the playground, where the *Royal Ashcrumb*'s original figurehead—a large, creepy-looking bronze mermaid that had decorated the prow of the ship—lay, her tail half buried in the earth. The mermaid was the favorite piece of playground equipment among the first graders, but they wouldn't slide down her slimy scales today. Outdoor recess, Misty guessed, was out of the question with this kind of weather, especially now that another dark cloud was moving toward the school.

"Good morning," Mr. Ableman said into the microphone. "As you all know, Halloween is this weekend."

Some students clapped and cheered.

Mr. Barrel yanked out his paddle the way a cowboy would flash a six-shooter and waved it at the audience. The crowd went quiet. He jammed it back into this pocket.

"Trick-or-treating is a lot of fun," continued Mr. Ableman.

"But you have to be careful! Mr. Barrel is going to give you some tips on how to be safe this Halloween."

Mr. Barrel threw his hands open wide and declared at the top of his lungs, "RAZOR BLADES IN APPLES! NAILS IN CHOCOLATE! LUMPS OF POISON!" He trotted to the side of the stage and pointed at a section of second graders. "That's right! There are weirdos who work around the clock, all year long, devising clever ways to disguise killer candy!"

Having achieved everyone's undivided attention, Mr. Barrel strolled back to the center of the stage, thunder rolling ominously.

As he began to read a list of trick-or-treating dos and don'ts, Misty glanced back at the playground. She scanned the stormy scenery, watching the seats of the swing sets pitch to and fro, the rain pelt the seesaws, and leaves scatter across the grass.

"DO NOT eat candy if the wrapper has been tampered with!" warned Mr. Barrel.

Misty squinted through the downpour. What was that lone figure standing beneath the trees? Dark and hunched, it hovered above the ground, moving slightly in the wind. As Misty watched it draw closer, she got the sinking feeling that it was watching *her*, too.

"DO NOT eat anything that smells or tastes like battery acid!" Mr. Barrel declared.

Trying to get a better view of the mysterious form on the playground, Misty leaned forward in her seat.

In an instant, the thing sprang up, just outside the window.

Misty screamed, but not as loudly as Mr. Barrel.

"WHAT *IS* THAT?" the vice principal shouted, clutching his chest.

Shrieks filled the room as the entire assembly spied the creature leaning against the windowpane, its long hair bristling in the wind and rain. They jumped to their feet, craning to see it better.

"It's hairy!"

"It's floating!"

"It ain't got a head!"

"It *doesn't* have a head," a teacher corrected. "And it doesn't have any feet, either!"

Mr. Ableman thumped the microphone in an attempt to get the frantic group's attention. "Calm down!" he blared. "Back to your seats. Now!"

The group reluctantly followed his orders, whispering hysterically as they fumbled for their chairs. Returning to her seat, Misty knew there was something about the figure that seemed familiar.

"I'm going to see what this is all about," said Mr. Ableman.

"B-b-be careful," warned Mr. Barrel, his eyes glued upon the creature.

Mr. Ableman marched to the side door, flung it open, and ventured outside. Everyone watched in nervous silence as the principal approached the mysterious figure. By the way his head bobbed, one could tell Mr. Ableman was shouting, though nothing could be heard over the steady downpour of rain.

"It's leaving!" someone cried as the dark form backed away from the window and hurried off.

Mr. Ableman, knowing all eyes were on him, shook his fist one more time and headed back into the building.

"Show's over!" he announced as he sloshed indoors, completely drenched.

"What was it?" said Mr. Barrel.

"Um—well, uh," stammered Mr. Ableman. "Er—it appears to be just some matty old dog."

While the older students groaned, saddened that the drama had ended, the younger ones sighed in relief and emerged from their hiding places. A few first graders remained under tables, sobbing and shaking, some even sucking their thumbs while teachers tried to coax them out.

"In conclusion, there is much to fear about Halloween," said Mr. Ableman. "Assembly dismissed. Back to your classes."

The rest of the school day was blown. No one believed the dog explanation, and everyone was so alarmed about the "playground beast" that nobody could concentrate. Even the teachers couldn't quit looking out the window. By the time the bell rang signaling everybody to go home, nobody had the guts. What if the hairy thing was waiting for them?

Margie Medford offered little comfort for the students as they faced their journeys home. "RUN!" she yelled. "Run home as fast as you can!"

Like racehorses out of the starting gate, the children exploded onto the street, dashing down the sidewalk, their eyes as big as pies. Misty and Yoshi were among them, bumbling along with their huge umbrella.

"Just a little farther," Yoshi told Misty. "Then we'll be home."

Misty stopped in her tracks. That's it! Suddenly, she realized where she had seen the hairy, armless, footless, and headless form before.

"Fannie Belcher's coat!" she gasped.

"What?" said Yoshi. "What are you talking about?"

"I think it's time I told you my secret," said Misty.

3

May Nays

One hour and an entire box of cookies later, Misty had finished telling Yoshi about her mysterious experience at Madame Zaster's house and Fannie Belcher's diary and coat.

Yoshi sat on Misty's bed, exhausted from listening and eating.

"Incredible," decided Yoshi, her mouth covered with crumbs.

"I didn't tell my family, because I knew they wouldn't believe me," said Misty, straightening her glasses. "But you believe me . . . don't you?"

Before Yoshi could answer, a loud thump sounded from the desk drawer.

"What's that?" Yoshi whispered.

"It's Fannie Belcher's old diary," said Misty shakily.

"*Really?*" said Yoshi, her eyes glittering. "That diary really wants to get out of there, doesn't it?"

"Yeah," said Misty. "But it's not going anywhere. I locked the drawer."

"You know what I think?" said Yoshi in a hushed voice. "I think Fannie Belcher hid that diary in the phone, and it's trying to escape because it doesn't want to be read. Yeah, I bet it contains Fannie Belcher's deepest secrets . . . secrets that she never intended to share."

"That might explain Fannie Belcher's coat stalking around," guessed Misty. "Maybe it's trying to get the diary back. I really think that coat is stalking me! I swear I felt like it was looking at me through the window at assembly."

The diary slammed against the drawer, and the girls jumped.

"What should we do?" asked Misty.

"I think we should read it," answered Yoshi excitedly. "It might reveal some explanation for all the weird stuff going on."

"Okay," said Misty, unlocking the drawer. "Here it goes."

The moment she pulled open the drawer, the diary flew from the compartment, bounced off the ceiling, and landed on the floor, where it began flopping about like a fish out of water.

Yoshi jumped up and down on the bed screaming, "Get it! Get it!"

FOOM!—Misty nailed the diary with a pillow, knocking her glasses from her face. The diary darted toward her, grazing her ear. Misty ducked, then leapt forward. *CRUNCH!*—her glasses shattered beneath her feet.

"My glasses!" Misty groaned, really swinging at the diary now. A few more clumsy *FWOPS* from the feather pillow, and the book rose into the air, flicked its pages at Misty, and dropped onto the bed. It twitched for a moment, then went still.

"What's going on in there?" Mrs. Gordon called from the hallway.

"Nothing!" Misty replied.

"I think you knocked it out," whispered Yoshi. "Better read it while we have the chance."

The girls sat on the bed. Misty bravely took the diary into her lap and opened it. She squinted at the first page. "You're going to have to read it," she told Yoshi. "Without my glasses, I can't see a thing."

"Okay," said Yoshi, leaning over to read. "Hmm, there's no date for the entry, but judging by how old these pages are, it's an entry from a long, long time ago. Anyway, this is what it says:

"A clairvoyant by the name of Madame Zaster has moved into a cottage on Shadow Street. Since none of us three Descendants knew if the Golden Three had been destroyed or were in fact buried in Ashcrumb, we thought we might see if Madame Zaster might be able to help us."

"Descendants?" blurted Misty. "What does Fannie Belcher mean by Descendants?"

"How should I know?" said Yoshi, irritated. "And don't interrupt!"

Yoshi continued reading.

"So we three Descendants paid Madame Zaster a visit. She led us to her séance table and asked us to sit and hold hands while she gazed into her crystal ball.

"Hazel Monger, always impatient, was in no mood to wait for Madame Zaster to 'see' anything. 'Don't waste our time with a hocus-pocus show!' Hazel shouted at Zaster. 'Just tell us about the Golden Three! Are they buried in Ashcrumb?'

"Madame Zaster peered into the crystal ball. We Descendants couldn't see a thing, but evidently she could. Slowly, she nodded and spoke a riddle—"

"Misty!" Mrs. Gordon called. Misty slammed the diary shut and tossed it back into the desk drawer.

"What?" wailed Misty.

"Remember, you have to babysit at the Sweethouses' tonight," said her mother. "Don't be late!"

"Great," Misty grumbled to Yoshi. "I totally forgot that I had to babysit tonight."

"That's the least of your problems," Yoshi said, pointing to Misty's mangled glasses. "You'll have to wear your spares."

"Those *were* my spares," Misty said.

"Wait a second," remembered Yoshi. "Didn't you say that you could see out of Madame Zaster's eyeglasses?"

"Oh, yeah," said Misty. "I guess I could wear those until I get another pair."

Misty took Madame Zaster's cat-eye glasses from the vanity and slipped them on.

Yoshi roared with laughter.

"Do they look that bad?" asked Misty, the pointy tips of the thick-rimmed glasses sticking out from her hair.

"No, no," said Yoshi, clearing her throat. "They're actually very retro."

"MISTY!" Mrs. Gordon called again. "You're going to be late!"

"Not if I take the Vespa," Misty yelled back.

"The Vespa?" said Yoshi. "Did your dad finally get that old thing to run?"

"Kinda," said Misty. "It's still backfiring and stalling pretty badly."

"Okay, well, I'm going home," said Yoshi. "We'll read more of the diary tomorrow." Halfway out Misty's door, Yoshi turned. "Hey, I wonder if the Hazel Monger who Fannie Belcher was talking about in the diary is the same Hazel Monger who lives down the street?"

"Hazel Monger, the freaky hermit?" said Misty. "I bet it is! After all, how can there be more than one Hazel Monger in town?"

Misty glimpsed her reflection in the vanity mirror and sighed. "These glasses look awful."

"Cheer up," giggled Yoshi as Misty locked the desk drawer. "At least you're babysitting for the Sweethouses. At least *that's* some good news!"

It was good news for a couple of reasons. First, the Sweethouses owned a candy and condiment supply company, which meant their house was filled to the brim with every imaginable candy and food spread known to humankind. Just in their kitchen pantry alone, they had enough chocolate and ketchup to feed a small country. Second, their child was a babysitter's dream. Nicknamed Sweetpea, he was a sluggish nine-month-old baby who slept all the time. Which meant less time having to actually babysit and more time for raiding the pantry.

Thunder was rumbling as Misty set off on the Vespa. An antique motor scooter, the banged-up red Vespa wasn't the smoothest or most reliable ride, but it did come in handy sometimes, and for the moment, it was behaving fine.

Drizzle began to fall as Misty motored slowly down the street, nearing the Monger mansion. Though four families could have lived easily within the mansion, it was home to just one person: Hazel Monger. Without a doubt, Hazel was the most loathsome person in town. She hated children and kept a bag of rocks with her at all times, just in case some child trespassed onto her lawn.

Misty glanced at the home's vast front porch. There sat one-hundred-year-old Hazel Monger in the flesh, rocking slowly in her creaky, old rocking chair. The woman's snaky eyes followed Misty as she drove past the mansion's iron gate.

Then, without warning—

KA-POW!

—the Vespa backfired, the explosive noise sending Hazel Monger straight up out of her chair.

"Get out of here!" Hazel Monger screeched, rattling her bag of rocks.

Misty gulped as the Vespa coughed miserably and sputtered slowly forward. "Oh no," groaned Misty. "Don't conk out now!"

"Nasty little brats, always spying on me!" Hazel yelled, flinging some rocks at Misty. "Always coming around my house! Trying to sniff out my secret!"

Misty quickly throttled the gas. With a jolt, the Vespa took off and didn't stop until reaching the Sweethouses' home.

"Hello, Misty," Mrs. Sweethouse said, opening the door. "Well, look at those new glasses!"

"Oh, these things?" said Misty, pushing the cat-eye glasses up the bridge of her nose. "They're just temporary."

Mrs. Sweethouse glanced at the boiling sky. "It's lightning again? This rain just doesn't want to stop. I've never seen anything like it."

Misty walked inside and smiled. It was a wonderful house, very cozy, with matching sofas and chairs, all situated around the biggest television she'd ever seen.

"I've left emergency telephone numbers on the refrigerator," said Mrs. Sweethouse as her husband came into the room. "Sweetpea is asleep already," she continued, buttoning her coat. "Oh, and his baby monitor is on the sofa. Everything should be just fine. The pantry's stocked, so make yourself at home, and we'll be back before nine o'clock." Then they were gone.

Misty trotted into the living room, kicked off her shoes, and collapsed on the mushy sofa. The Sweethouses' terrier appeared, barking to be picked up.

"Shh," Misty said. "You'll wake the baby." He pawed at her hand. He was always begging for food.

"Are you hungry?" Misty asked.

The dog wagged his tail.

"Then follow me. I know where we can find the good stuff."

The terrier padded alongside Misty as she shuffled to the kitchen's enormous walk-in pantry and flipped on the light.

"Jackpot," she grinned, gazing at the amazing display of junk food. Every square inch of the room was filled with something that could either rot your teeth or your stomach. Huge boxes filled with chocolates stood stacked on shelves. Bags stuffed with hard candies, taffies, chewing gums, and jawbreakers leaned against the wall. Sitting on the floor were tall, industrial-size barrels of pickles, mustard, and other food spreads, often seen in the kitchen of Ashcrumb Elementary's cafeteria.

Atop a shelf a radio played. *"More thunderstorms headed our way,"* the announcer said smoothly. *"Expect heavy showers and severe lightning throughout the evening. Looks like it's going to be another stormy night for Ashcrumb!"*

"Ah, here's something for you," Misty told the terrier, handing him a doggie treat. "And here's something for me," she said happily, scooping up some chocolates. Her pockets filled, she returned to the couch and turned on the TV.

Dracula was playing. Misty tossed some candy in her mouth, chewing nervously as she watched the vampire creep across the screen, his eyes gleaming hungrily as he stalked a visitor inside his castle.

Misty picked up the baby monitor and held it to her ear. She could hear the hushed breathing of the baby, deep in sleep. "Sounds like he's out for the night," she said, laying the monitor back down.

Thunder rumbled, and rain began pelting the window. Misty huddled deep into the couch and cringed as Dracula exposed his fangs, lifted his cape, and swooped upon his hapless victim.

The telephone rang. Misty fumbled for it.

"Hello?"

"Hey, it's me," came Yoshi's anxious voice on the other end.

"Hey," said Misty. "Do you want to come over?"

"No. Listen," Yoshi said in a rush. "There's been a breakout at the asylum."

"Right," Misty laughed, guessing this was some kind of joke.

"It's true!" Yoshi yelled. "You've got to believe me! The police are looking for—"

"Looking for what?" Misty said, playing along. "Looking for what?" Misty blinked. "Hello? Yoshi, are you there?"

But it was no use. The phone line had gone dead. As dead as the blood-drained person lying on Dracula's castle floor.

As Misty tried Yoshi's number, a noise came over the baby monitor that made Misty's heart skip a beat. It was the sound of a window shattering.

Misty gasped, sitting bolt upright, her heart thumping in her throat. The dog growled, hackles rising on his back.

Misty grabbed the monitor and pressed it to her ear. An icy chill came over her as she listened in utter terror to another sound, the sound of low grunts and footsteps.

Someone had broken into the house.

"The baby," Misty whispered in panic. "I've got to get the baby!" She jumped from the couch and dashed toward the baby's room, only to see the frightening shadow of an intruder moving down the hall. To Misty's relief, the intruder had already passed up the baby's room, but to Misty's *alarm*, it was headed right toward *her*.

Run! Misty heard herself screaming inside her head. *Run and hide!* Misty turned on her heels and bolted to the kitchen, skidding inside its huge pantry. She slammed the door and looked frantically around the dim room. Where could she hide?

Spying the barrels, Misty dropped to the floor and scooted behind them, drawing her knees to her chest and backing herself against the wall. Over the pounding of her heart, she heard an announcement from the radio:

"*We interrupt this broadcast for some breaking news. A patient has just escaped from the Ashcrumb Mental Facility! This man is considered extremely unstable! Police are presently searching for him, so stay inside and keep your doors locked! We will keep you updated as the events unfold. Now, back to our regular programming.*"

As a song began playing, Misty peeked through the gap between the barrels. Except for a sliver of light from the kitchen passing underneath the pantry door, the room was almost completely dark. Though Misty couldn't see anything, she could *hear* everything going on inside the house. She bit her lip as the terrier's barking sounded from the living room.

Another wave of panic washed over Misty as the grunts and footsteps grew louder. Just then, as if a tornado was spinning through the kitchen, pots and pans began crashing to the floor and cabinet doors started slamming. She heard the refrigerator door open and its contents tumble to the floor.

What is that maniac doing? thought Misty. She shut her eyes tight, as if she were riding a roller coaster. The sensation was just the same, for here came the sick, stomach-dropping feeling as the pantry door flew open.

Panting and snorting, the intruder began tossing and shoving everything from the shelves. Bags exploded on the floor, boxes landed with deafening crashes, and cans clattered and rolled.

Don't make a sound! Misty told herself. She gagged as an awful stink filled the room. It smelled like the decaying stench of sour mud. Misty couldn't take it any longer. She *had* to look.

She opened her eyes and peeked again through the gap between the barrels. In the dim light, she could see the escapee's dirty institution pants and big, mud-covered feet. The crazy man's toes were right in front of her, twiddling excitedly. Evidently, something had caught the freak's attention. He breathed in heavily, grunting and groaning.

Can he see me? Misty wondered, keeping her head low.

"*More breaking news about the escapee from Ashcrumb Mental Facility!*" the radio announcer blared. "*This lunatic is known as May Nays!*"

Misty gulped, remembering what Yoshi had said about May Nays: *He will do anything to get his hands on mayonnaise. I mean . . . he'll kill for the stuff.*

Horror-struck, Misty read the label on the barrel behind which she was hiding. Apparently, the freak was reading it, too.

"MAYONNAISE!" his gargled voice erupted. Misty gasped as his filthy hands crept around the sides of the barrel. "ME FOUND MAYONNAISE!"

Misty was just about to bolt when the rims of her eyeglasses grew instantly cold. Their lenses fogged over, as if she were passing through a mist. Yet she could still see perfectly through them. And what did she see through the gap but Madame Zaster's ghost, floating by the pantry door.

In its eerie, static-y voice, the ghost declared, "*Misty, stay where you are . . . and move only when I say!*"

Against all reason, Misty obeyed, keeping her body still and her eyes fixed on the ghost.

"MAYONNAISE!" the escapee laughed wildly, tugging on the barrel. "GIMME! GIMME!"

At any moment, the barrel would slide out, and Misty would be doomed.

"*Run now!*" the apparition suddenly called. "*Hurry!*"

Out dashed Misty, catching May Nays off guard.

"Rarrrr!" he growled, making a swipe at Misty.

"*This way!*" Madame Zaster's ghost wailed, beckoning from the pantry doorway.

Her heart racing, Misty rushed out of the pantry, slid through the kitchen, and raced down the hall to the baby's room. He was still sleeping! Misty swept him up into her arms and climbed out the window.

Outside the rain fell in torrents. Her ears ringing with fear, Misty sprinted across the wet yard and down the street, candy dropping from her pockets as she ran.

4

The Riddle

By the time the police reached May Nays that night, he had eaten two barrels of his favorite sludge. Covered from head to toe in the white goop, the bloated and sluggish May Nays was led from the Sweethouses' home by the sheriff, Dr. Yamamoto, and ten big nurses.

A group of whispering adults watched from across the street as the barefoot May Nays hobbled down the Sweethouses' sidewalk, the terrier licking at his greasy heels as he slipped and slid to the asylum's waiting van.

"Thank goodness the baby is okay," one of the onlookers mumbled, nodding toward Mrs. Sweethouse, who stood in her front doorway, clutching her infant.

"What about the babysitter?" another person asked.

"She's fine. After narrowly escaping May Nays, she rescued the baby!" answered a police officer scribbling in a notepad. "I questioned her and sent her home with her family."

The group watched in silence as the van backed out of the driveway with May Nays's shiny face gazing out the window, sticking out his tongue at the terrier, who trailed behind the vehicle, barking its head off. After the van rumbled away, the crowd dispersed, and everyone headed back home. Within minutes, the street was quiet again, as if nothing had happened at all.

However, things were just getting started for Misty on her drive home. She sat in the front seat between her parents, listening to them declare, "Thank goodness you're alive!" over and over again, while James bombarded her with a million questions from the backseat. "What did May Nays smell like? What kind of grunt did he make? A pig grunt or a gorilla grunt?"

"Thank goodness you're alive!" bellowed Mr. Gordon, giving Misty a crushing side hug.

"What did his toes look like?" James asked breathlessly. "Were they fat sausage toes? Or were they crooked, crazy toes?"

"Thank goodness you're alive!" sobbed Mrs. Gordon. "It's a miracle that you escaped, just a miracle!" She wiped her nose and shuddered.

"Well, it's all over now," said Mr. Gordon in a consoling tone. "It's all over."

Misty felt as if she were sleepwalking as she climbed out of the car and trudged inside her house. She was so exhausted that her legs felt as if they were made of rubber.

Misty dropped onto her bed and fell fast asleep. No amount of bumping from the diary could wake her *that* night.

"Check it out!" James said the next morning at breakfast. "Misty made the front page of the newspaper!"

"Our little Misty is a celebrity, ay?" Mr. Gordon said, spreading the *Daily Ashcrumb* on the table and having a look. Misty peeked over his shoulder.

"No way!" she gasped, reading the headline:

HOLD THE MAYO!

ASYLUM ESCAPEE MAY NAYS CAPTURED!

LOCAL BABYSITTER HERO! BABY SAFE!

"Your picture is grotesque!" laughed James, pointing at the photo of Misty.

Her jaw dropped when she saw the picture. It very well could have been the worst photograph ever taken of her. It had been snapped while the police officer was questioning her. Her hair hung in stringy clumps, and her wet socks were so stretched out that they looked like clown shoes. To make matters worse, the picture had been taken right when Misty was pushing Madame Zaster's glasses up the bridge of her nose. From the angle of the shot, it appeared that Misty's index finger was going straight up her nostril.

"You were picking your nose?" chuckled James. "You're so busted!"

"I wasn't picking my nose," Misty yelled, thumping him on the ear.

"Say," said Mr. Gordon, prodding the newspaper with a butter knife. "Here's the latest news on that creature that was spotted at Ashcrumb Elementary yesterday. Says here in the paper that it was probably a Halloween prank."

"I don't care what the paper says," said James, shaking his head. "It wasn't a prank. The playground beast is real! You should have seen it, Dad!"

"Well," said Mrs. Gordon as she stared out the kitchen window at the drizzle. "All I know is that things are getting weird in Ashcrumb."

"Weird?" coughed James. "Don't you mean *weirder*? This town is a freak zone."

"True, it's always been odd," agreed Mrs. Gordon. "But I think it's strange how so many things are happening. The sighting at the school. This terrible weather, and that horrible May Nays escaping."

If she only knew the half of it! thought Misty.

"Speaking of May Nays," James grinned. "Look at this."

James opened his grungy backpack, pulled out a glass jar, and placed it on the table. It was filled with water and an unidentifiable floating object.

"What in the world is that?" asked Mr. Gordon, tapping on the jar with his fork.

"It's May Nays's toe," said James. "At least, that's what I'm saying at school. It's really a Vienna sausage. I stuck one of Mom's fake fingernails in it to make it look more authentic." James smiled proudly at his revolting creation. "I'm going to charge the first graders a dollar to look at it."

Misty grimaced.

"See," James explained to his sister, "I'm going to tell everybody you chopped May Nays's toe off. If you go along with my story, then I'll split the money with you."

"That's my little businessman!" cheered Mr. Gordon. "You've got quite a head on your shoulders, son! Now, where were those obituaries?"

While Mr. Gordon hunted through the newspaper for the names of the dead and James sloshed the "toe" around in the jar, Misty met Yoshi outside.

"Are you all right?" said Yoshi. "You look sick."

"You'd look sick, too, if your picture was plastered on the front page of the newspaper," Misty said morosely.

"Well, I wouldn't worry about it," said Yoshi as they moved down the sidewalk. "My dad says you were really lucky to have escaped. How *did* you escape, anyway? The newspaper didn't explain that part."

"That's because I didn't *tell* them that part," replied Misty. "They wouldn't have believed me."

Misty looked around to make sure that James wasn't following. Then she took a deep breath and told Yoshi how the cat-eye glasses had turned cold and how Madame Zaster's ghost had helped her escape.

"Do you know what this means?" whispered Yoshi. "This means that Madame Zaster totally saved your life!"

"I know, but why?" said Misty. Then she tapped on the cat-eye glasses she was wearing. "And why did these glasses grow cold?"

"I haven't the foggiest idea," said Yoshi. "But maybe, just maybe, the glasses grew cold because you were about to see into another dimension. The dimension that Madame Zaster exists in. The dimension of ghosts."

Misty shivered. "How do you know about all that creepy stuff?"

"Because we have computers at our house," Yoshi said matter-of-factly. "There's all sorts of material on that kind of stuff. I swear, Misty, your family has *got* to get a computer!"

"Dad doesn't like computers," mumbled Misty.

"Oh, that's right . . . I forgot," said Yoshi, remembering her manners. Yoshi knew the real reason the Gordons didn't have a computer was because they couldn't afford one. "I'm still freaked out about Fannie Belcher's diary," said Yoshi, changing the subject. "Have you had a chance to read any more of it?"

"No. But I did hear it thumping in my desk this morning."

"We'll have to read more of it this afternoon," said Yoshi.

Up ahead, Margie Medford waved her STOP sign. Misty sighed. Just thinking about how she'd be taunted about the May Nays incident and her pathetic picture in the paper gave Misty butterflies in her stomach. *I could either turn around and run back home or march forward and face misery*, Misty thought to herself just as Medford caught sight of them.

Misty didn't have a chance to decide. The crossing guard was on top of the girls.

"Move it, move it, move it, you bunch of pea-brains!" Medford called, brandishing her STOP sign like a sword fighter.

The girls joined the bustling herd of students and stampeded quickly across the street, leaving little Jimmy Winn behind, his pink ears drawing Medford's attention.

Medford rushed up to Jimmy and cuffed him on both ears, sending him rolling into some bushes.

Good grief, gulped Misty. Was this terror a foreshadowing of things to come? What horrors awaited *her* inside school? Her newspaper picture! And her nutty cat-eye glasses! She was doomed!

She ducked inside the school, nervously drawing her hands up and down the strap of her bag, waiting for the teasing to begin. She didn't have to wait long, for here came Alexis Lenox and her smirking friends.

"*Nice* glasses, hero!" jeered Alexis, giving Misty a poke in the ribs. "We all just *loved* your picture in the paper!"

Misty and Yoshi turned away and headed in the opposite direction.

"Hey, vulture!" called Alexis loudly, causing people at their lockers to look. "I got a message for you . . . HOLD THE MAYO!"

Snickers passed through the hall as Misty waded past, keeping her head down.

"Don't let it get to you," said Yoshi.

But that was easier said than done. Try as she might to concentrate in her morning classes—while Mrs. Hale, the math teacher, went over equations, and then in social studies, when Mrs. Lane discussed the origin of the jack-o'-lantern—Misty couldn't get the recent bizarre events out of her mind. And as if discovering a freaky diary, meeting a ghost, being stalked by a haunted mink coat, and then being attacked by an asylum escapee weren't enough, she had to contend with jeering at school.

At recess, Misty and Yoshi went to a place on the school grounds far from everyone, and they sat underneath a large maple tree, whose large boughs and remaining autumn leaves provided privacy from the likes of Alexis Lenox.

"So, what are you going to do for Halloween?" Yoshi asked.

"I'm going to take James and Hector trick-or-treating," Misty answered, drawing in the mud with a stick. "Want to come?"

"Yeah, sure," said Yoshi. "Hey, there goes James right now! He looks like he's in trouble."

Misty spun around to see her brother being yanked across the playground by a teacher.

"Scaring the wits out of those poor little boys and girls," the teacher was scolding James, "with that . . . that . . . toe in the jar!"

"It's a sausage!" insisted James, holding the jar out of the teacher's reach. "It's nothin' but a sausage, man!"

"Well, you can explain that to Vice Principal Barrel in his office," she snapped, dragging James inside.

"It looks like James and I are both having a bad day," Misty said, shaking her head.

Unfortunately for Misty, the rest of the school day didn't get any better. Mr. Marsh, the science teacher, made everyone in Misty's class dissect a frog. Then Mrs. Williams, who taught both English and art, had the students write a descriptive paper on the hairy playground beast and then sketch a drawing of it. PE was a disaster. Misty and her classmates had to run four laps around the castle, while Coach Knuckles followed alongside in his golf cart yelling, "Come on now, let's hustle! Pick up the pace!"

After school, it was obvious on the walk home that James Gordon had no intention of picking up *his* pace. He knew that as soon as he walked through his door, he'd have to face his parents, who'd gotten a fuming phone call from Vice Principal Barrel regarding the "toe in the jar."

Slow as his feet moved, however, the wheels in James's mind were moving at breakneck speed, working on an elaborate ploy to avoid punishment.

"Hey," James called over his shoulder to Misty and Yoshi. "Does this limp look real?" He took a step, dragged his right foot, and hobbled a bit.

"Yeah, I guess," said Yoshi. "You kinda look like the hunchback of Notre Dame."

"Don't blow my cover," James told Misty as they reached their house. "This fake limp is my only hope. I'm gonna tell

Mom and Dad I sprained my ankle. If they think I'm really hurt, then they'll forget everything. I can't risk being grounded on Halloween."

"Okay, okay," agreed Misty. "But you owe me one."

James's act worked. Not only did his parents forgive him his visit to the vice principal's office, but he was babied and fussed over at dinner by his mother, who truly believed he had twisted his ankle in a mud puddle.

"You poor boy," Mrs. Gordon said, sympathetically. "Here, have some more mashed potatoes."

"And if it will make you feel any better," added Mr. Gordon, rubbing James's head, "you can pick out a costume for Halloween from the Dearly Departed."

Realizing that he was home free, James gave Misty a side-glance and grinned. Misty felt a flicker of anger burn in her throat.

"I can't believe this," blurted Misty. "Has everyone forgotten that I almost got killed by an asylum escapee? Honestly!" She glared at her mom and dad. "Last night I narrowly escaped death and you barely even talk about it today, and then James gets a stupid limp and he gets rewarded!"

"Sweetie, that isn't true," said her mother.

"Yes, it is," said Misty. "By the way, have any of you even *noticed* that I'm wearing a totally different pair of glasses?"

"I have," chuckled James. "You must have excavated those things from the Crypt of Ugly!"

"Crypt of Ugly?" said Mrs. Gordon. "Is that a new brand?"

Misty rolled her eyes. "Good grief."

"Now, now, Misty," said Mr. Gordon, sensing an explosion brewing at the table. "Don't be silly! We haven't forgotten you! Tell you what," he added, holding a hunk of meat loaf in the air, "just to cheer you up, you can pick out a costume from the Dearly Departed, too!"

"I'm nearly too old for trick-or-treating, Dad," Misty said dully.

"Well, you can still take your brother to the store Saturday morning and let him pick out a costume. Mr. Yates will help you."

Mr. Yates was the sleepy manager of the Dearly Departed Antiques Store. Ninety-nine years old, Mr. Yates lived in the back room of the shop and spent his time in the store dusting, yawning, and snoozing on couches or piles of collectable newspapers. He was always falling asleep in the store window, drawing crowds of onlookers, who thought he was made of wax. But who could blame Mr. Yates for dozing off in the store? It wasn't exactly an exciting place, which is why Misty and James rarely visited it.

As the Gordons were finishing their dessert, there was a knock at the front door.

"I'll get it," said Misty, getting up. "It's just Yoshi. We're going to do some homework in my room."

"Hi, everybody!" Yoshi hollered a little too brightly as she trotted inside with an armload of books. "Just came to do a little math and English. Got to keep up with the schoolwork, you know."

"Don't push it," whispered Misty, nudging Yoshi toward her room. "They'll know we're up to something."

The girls went to Misty's room and locked the door.

The diary was thumping wildly inside the desk.

"How are we going to read the diary with it going crazy like that?" asked Yoshi.

"We're just gonna have to knock it out again," said Misty boldly. "You open the drawer, and I'll hit it with this thing," Misty said, picking up Fannie Belcher's phone.

"Ready?" said Yoshi, turning the key in the drawer lock.

Misty nodded, and Yoshi opened the drawer. Out shot the diary, and Misty hit it with the phone, knocking the dust out of the book with a loud clang and sending it to the floor.

"Nice swing!" said Yoshi.

"Thanks," said Misty, nudging the book with her foot. "It's definitely out." She picked up the diary, and the girls sat on the bed.

"So, where were we?" Misty said.

"Well," recalled Yoshi as Misty opened the book, "Hazel Monger, who is one of the 'Descendants,' had just asked

Madame Zaster if the Golden Three—whatever they are—were buried in Ashcrumb."

"Right," said Misty, picking up from the place where'd they'd left off the day before:

"Madame Zaster peered into the crystal ball. We Descendants couldn't see a thing, but evidently she could. Slowly, she nodded and spoke a riddle:

> *'When English garb did fool the county,*
> *Snakes passed in with royal bounty:*
> *The ancient and mighty Golden Three,*
> *With powers to rule the earth, sky, and sea.*

> *'Into a storm the Three were tossed,*
> *With fire and rain, they all were lost.*
> *Still they lie, their heads sunken deep,*
> *In a forgotten place, still they sleep.*

> *'But beware—Hark! Listen well,*
> *For with the solitary gong of the Ashcrumb Bell,*
> *The Snakes' spirits will reclaim His Majesty's ship,*
> *Then from England begin their final trip.*

'There will be no stopping them, so lock your door!
Woe to Ashcrumb when the Snakes come ashore!
For they'll find the trio and harness their power,
They'll awaken the Dead, then kill and devour.'

"Madame Zaster had just finished speaking the riddle
when a young boy was seen at the window.

"'Someone is spying on us!' screamed Hazel Monger.
'I'll fix him!' She reached out of the window, grabbed the
boy, and—"

Just then, the diary jerked in Misty's hand. Quick as a blink,
she tossed the journal back into the desk drawer.

"What a freaky riddle," said Yoshi, enthralled. "I wonder what
the Golden Three could be."

Misty's eyes flew open. "Wait a second . . . Madame Zaster's
ghost spoke of the Golden Three when she appeared to me
in her cottage!" Misty paused as she remembered the ghost's
mysterious message. "She said, 'All will be revealed once you
have learned the nature of the Golden Three, but first you must
prove your nature to me.'" Misty scrunched up her nose. "I
wonder what she meant by 'nature'?"

"Well," said Yoshi, "my dad is always talking about people's nature. It's their character, basically. You know . . . like it's Margie Medford's nature to be a bully . . . or Hazel Monger's nature to be mean. But," she added, squinting thoughtfully, "since we don't know what the Golden Three are, nature for them might have to do with natural phenomena . . . like 'forces of nature' kinda stuff."

"Whatever the Golden Three are," said Misty, locking the drawer, "it sounds like they can do some pretty terrifying things."

"Awaken the dead, kill, and devour," said Yoshi jokingly, with a spooky tone in her voice, but Misty wasn't much amused. There was something about the riddle that made her very uneasy.

"Who do you think the Snakes are?" asked Yoshi. "And that boy—that boy who was spying on the séance—I wonder who he was."

"Who knows?" said Misty. "But I'll tell you one thing, we're going to get to the bottom of it."

5

The Dearly Departed

Wake up! It's Halloween!" James shouted, prodding Misty's pillow. "You gotta take me to get my costume at the Dearly Departed!"

"What?" drooled Misty, half asleep. "Why can't you just walk there yourself?"

"What? Are you crazy?" he yelled. "The playground beast might get me!"

"I wish," Misty sighed.

She also later wished that she had worn a jacket for their walk to the Dearly Departed. Though it was sunny, it was extremely chilly and windy, the biting gusts tinged with salt from the nearby ocean. The wind hadn't kept people indoors that brisk

Saturday morning, though. Plenty of shoppers, mostly tourists, were out and about on cobblestoned Plunder Street, enjoying its various shops, restaurants, and pubs, with backs banked along the seashore.

As usual, a big crowd stood in front of the Ashcrumb Museum. In addition to many historical artifacts displayed within its main building, the museum featured quite a tourist attraction: an underwater walking tunnel that stretched from the interior of the museum all the way down to the bottom of the bay, where, through a window, sightseers could view the gloomy, barnacle-encrusted, sunken remnants of the ship, the *Royal Ashcrumb.*

Next to the museum stood the ancient stone Bell Tower, at whose top the Ashcrumb Bell hung—which centuries ago had signaled the arrival of the ship.

Misty glanced up at the bell. She got a prickly feeling as she recalled its mention in the strange riddle. *Beware! Hark, and listen well, for with the solitary gong of the Ashcrumb Bell . . .*

Fat chance, thought Misty, *that the bell would ever ring again, considering that it was damaged in the same legendary storm that destroyed the ship.*

Misty and James scooted through the group of tourists and continued down the sidewalk, passing neat little storefronts, whose windows were decorated with scarecrows, orange streamers, and twinkling lights. Large carts of pumpkins perfect for carving jack-o'-lanterns stood outside Harkin's Hardware. In the window of the elegant Optical Illusion Eyeglass Shop, a display of lifelike owls and cats wearing glasses seemed to wink at passersby. Next door, in front of Sweethouse Candy and Condiments Shop, a woman dressed as a witch handed out treats to children.

"Misty?" said the witch, turning with basket in hand. "Happy Halloween!"

Misty squinted at the witch, trying to recognize the person under the black pointy hat and bright green makeup. "Mrs. Sweethouse?"

The witch nodded.

"So, how are you feeling after . . . after . . ." Mrs. Sweethouse hesitated. "Well, *you know*." Mrs. Sweethouse leaned down and whispered in Misty's ear. "The May Nays incident?"

"Fine," said Misty. "Really."

"Glad to hear it," said Mrs. Sweethouse. "I just don't know how we could ever repay you for saving our little Sweetpea!" She gave Misty a hug and then tapped the thick rims of Misty's glasses. "I'm still getting used to seeing you wear those things."

"Me too," said Misty. "Well, we need to be getting to the Dearly Departed. James is picking out a costume for trick-or-treating."

"Remember to pay my house a visit tonight," Mrs. Sweethouse said to James, handing him some candy. "And that goes for you, too, Misty!"

Misty and James scurried past the Blacksmith Shoppe, Sinclair's Sea Store, and finally the noisy Hum Rum Tavern, where its proprietor, Sam Port, stood in the doorway, polishing a drinking mug with the hem of his apron. "Lookin' for Mr. Yates?" said Mr. Port.

The red-nosed Mr. Port took a few steps out of his tavern's doorway and pointed to the Dearly Departed's window. Behind its smudged glass Mr. Yates lay, snoozing atop a Victorian couch.

"Thanks, Mr. Port," sighed Misty, opening the shop's door and pushing James inside.

Bells tinkled, and Mr. Yates snorted awake, yelling out of habit, "Welcome to the Dearly Departed!"

James snickered, while Misty helped Mr. Yates out of the window and onto the floor of the shop.

"Why, it's the young Gordons!" Mr. Yates cried, rubbing his watery eyes behind his glasses. "What brings you to the store?" he added, blowing a cloud of dust from a stack of books.

"I'm here to find a Halloween costume," said James, sneezing.

"Ah, Halloween! So that's what today is," Mr. Yates mused, taking off his hat and scratching his silver-haired head. "I thought we were still in the month of August . . ." His voice trailed off for a moment, and he put his hat back on. "But it's Halloween, you say?" He glanced out the window and nodded. "Well, that explains the chilly weather and all those bloomin' pumpkins on the street!"

James and Misty shook their heads. Mr. Yates had a terrible memory. His memory was so bad that in order to keep from losing his keys, he wore them on a chain around his neck. Oddly, Mr. Yates could remember things that had occurred fifty years ago, but he couldn't recall what he had eaten for lunch. He would tell you something and then two minutes later— presto!—the thought would vanish, and he wouldn't even remember having spoken to you. Hard-pressed as he was to remember the present, he had a passion for the past, and you could not find a kinder gentleman or one as knowledgeable about antiques as dear Mr. Yates.

While James inspected a suit of armor, Misty wandered around the shop. To her astonishment, the store had actually gotten messier since her last visit. Books lay scattered atop dilapidated couches and faded chairs, cracked vases tottered on the edge of lopsided tables, and throughout the room a variety of broken floor lamps leaned against carved statues of tigers and monkeys. A velvet top hat lay on an open wardrobe, inside of which hung a red flapper dress from the 1920s, its fringe softly swaying in the drafty air. Collectable figurines—mostly thumb-size gnomes—seemed to pop up here and there, like spots before your eyes. Old paintings hung crooked against the walls, and in the dimmest corner of the room a carousel horse stood, its eyes wide and unblinking, as if equally astonished at the unbelievable display of junk.

Standing amidst the clutter, Misty spotted Madame Zaster's stained-glass floor lamp. She wondered, *Where are Madame Zaster's séance table, crystal ball, and chairs?* Her eyes searched the room for them, but they were nowhere to be found.

"Oh!" Mr. Yates yelped, as if a mouse had bitten him. "How about a little music?"

He trotted to a Victrola—a phonograph with a large, lily-shaped speaker—cranked its handle, and placed its needle on a thick black record. The "Charleston Rag" began playing.

"Dapper tune!" cheered Mr. Yates, dancing some clumsy steps, his wild kicks sending gnomes shooting across the floor.

Misty couldn't help laughing at Mr. Yates as he kidded around, waving his arms in the air and blowing kisses at the red flapper dress.

All of a sudden, Misty's laughter died. She sucked in her breath as she felt the cat-eye glasses growing painfully cold. In an instant, the lenses grew foggy. And what Misty saw next blew her mind.

Wearing the red flapper dress was the ghost of a woman,

completely decked out in 1920s style. Her bobbed hair swung back and forth as she danced and threw her translucent arms in the air. Misty gasped, stumbling backward into a lamp. She felt a tug on her sleeve. She spun around to behold another apparition, this one a pale blue man in a top hat and tuxedo, a life vest fastened about him. Shivering, the ghost held a boarding pass to the *Titanic*. "Could you direct me to the lifeboats?" he moaned.

Eerie laughter erupted from the corner of the room. Misty turned to see a ghastly little girl riding the carousel horse, shaking its reins in her milky white hands.

Misty let out a piercing scream.

"What's with you?" said James, still admiring the suit of armor. To Misty's horror, she saw that the gaps in the armor's face shield revealed the sickly, purple face of a knight. "Is the battle over?" the knight wailed, his hollow voice echoing inside the metal suit.

Misty bolted to her brother and snatched him away.

"Why are you freaking out?" James yelled.

"D-d-don't you see the knight in the armor?" asked Misty, trembling.

"Knight?" said James, a puzzled look on his face. "What are you talking about?"

"We're leaving right now," said Misty firmly.

"Are you kidding?" said James, exasperated. "I haven't even found a costume yet!"

Misty felt a tap on her shoulder. Warily, she looked. It was only Mr. Yates.

"Whatever is the matter?" he asked.

"We . . . we . . . ," Misty stammered, trying to remain calm despite seeing the ghost of a boy playing a game of marbles on the wooden floor. "We just have to be getting back home."

Misty gave James a warning look as if to say, *Don't even ask why*.

James sighed. "Bye, Mr. Yates."

"Wait! Wait just a moment," Mr. Yates said. "I'd like James to see something."

Mr. Yates opened the other side of the wardrobe and took out an ancient-looking garment. Made of old black leather, it had a V-shaped body, slightly puffed sleeves, and a long column of small brass buttons. Mr. Yates held it high in the air. "How about this doublet for a costume?" he asked James.

"Doublet?" said James. "What's a doublet?"

"A doublet is a type of jacket that European men wore between the fifteenth and seventeenth centuries," answered Mr. Yates. "This particular one is from England and happens to be authentic . . . and *not* for sale." Mr. Yates brushed a cobweb from it. "But you're more than welcome to wear it for Halloween."

James gazed at it. "I don't know," he said, scrunching up his nose. "I mean, it's cool looking and all, but it's way too big for me. And besides, I don't know if it's truly scary looking. Do you think it's scary enough for a Halloween costume, Misty?"

"Yes," she gulped. "*Definitely.*"

For Misty saw a ghost wearing the doublet. It was the smoky ghost of a grisly looking man, grimy with sweat and blood, a foul, burning smell oozing from him. Beneath his hat his long hair hung, dark and greasy and matted. On the side of his neck, just above his ruff, was a tattoo of a snake coiled around a skull. Beneath the skull were two tattooed words: *Black Adders.*

The horrid ghost squinted maliciously at Misty. Then it disappeared.

"Scary looking or not," Mr. Yates said as James looked at the doublet, "I think this English garb would make a very clever disguise."

Misty, who had been thinking nonstop of the mysterious riddle, mumbled, "When English garb did fool the county—"

"—Snakes passed in with royal bounty," declared Mr. Yates without missing a beat.

"*What* did you say?" Misty cried.

"When?" Mr. Yates said, biting his lip.

"Just now!" said Misty. "You said, 'Snakes passed in with royal bounty.'"

"Oh, did I?" Mr. Yates coughed, dropping the doublet and turning red. He grabbed his necklace and nervously rubbed an old skeleton key hanging from it. "Don't recall, don't recall. Well, good-bye, young Gordons!"

Mr. Yates quickly walked the siblings to the door and waved them out. He may as well have had a broom in his hand, shooing them as if they were two annoying cats.

Misty gave Mr. Yates a look over her shoulder as he closed the door behind them. There had been something in Mr. Yates's voice that led Misty to believe that he *did* remember what he'd just said.

He just didn't dare repeat it.

6

The Halloween Dare

The sun had just begun to set when something small, poufy, and pink appeared on the Gordons' front doorstep. It gave a few raps on the door and shrieked, "Trick or treat!"

"What have we here?" chirped Mrs. Gordon, opening the door.

Mr. Gordon stood next to his wife, with a large tray of candy in his hands. "Let me guess what you are," he smiled, leaning over the little girl. "A fairy?"

"No!" the girl screamed, jabbing Mr. Gordon in the leg with a crumpled orange sack. "I'm Cin-drella. Gimme some candy. Now!"

Afraid the child's mother might appear out of the bushes like a momma bear, Mr. Gordon chucked some candy in the girl's bag and shut the door.

James wandered down from his room wearing a gorilla mask.

"I see that you're ready for tonight," said Mrs. Gordon. "Where are the others?"

"Hector's on his way over right now," said James, his voice muffled. "And Misty and Yoshi are in Misty's room. They've been in there for hours."

Mrs. Gordon gazed at the rest of James's costume—a black sweater, jeans stained with black shoe polish, and shoes that were covered in thick brown fake fur.

"*Where* did you get that fur?" she asked.

"The bathroom rug," he replied.

"I thought so," she sighed, having wondered earlier how the bathroom rug had gotten a large bald patch. "Anyway, what's with the gorilla costume? You wore that last year. Why aren't you wearing something from the Dearly Departed?"

"Because I didn't have time to find anything there," James said, digging in the candy. "Misty made us leave. She freaked out in there."

"I can't hear a word you're saying," said Mr. Gordon, lifting the mask off James's face. "Did you say your sister freaked out in the store?"

"Yeah," said James. "She was falling over couches and tripping over junk. I tell ya, she was acting *really disturbed*."

"Disturbed?" said Mr. Gordon.

James nodded. "Yeah, she was seeing things, man. I've never seen her flip out like that before. And then, when Mr. Yates showed us an old doublet, she said something bizarre."

"Like what?" said Mr. Gordon.

James paused, crunching on a candy. "She said, 'When English garb did fool the county.' Yeah, that's what she said. And then Mr. Yates said something weird, too, something about some snakes coming with royal bounty."

Mr. Gordon sprang backward with a gasp.

"Dear?" Mrs. Gordon said to her husband. "What's the matter? You look funny. Are you all right?"

Mr. Gordon nodded slowly, as if in shock, with a faraway look in his eyes.

"Can I have my mask back now?" James asked, tugging it from his father's grasp.

James put the mask back on and joined his mother at the front door. While Mrs. Gordon waited for trick-or-treaters, James waited for Hector Figg, peeking out the window every few minutes for his friend.

Finally, Hector appeared at the front door in a black cape and fangs.

"Misty, Yoshi!" James called. "Hector's here. Let's go!"

James turned to grab his jacket from the coatrack.

That's when he saw his father, still standing in the same spot, his eyes huge and his mouth forming whispered words, as if he were working out a puzzle in his mind.

———

There are three types of houses worth visiting on Halloween. The first is the "trick-or-treat" variety. These are the houses that appear safe, with clean lawns and well-lighted porches, glowing jack-o'-lanterns, and plenty of candy. These are the houses that parents approve of. The Sweethouses' home is of the "trick-or-treat" variety.

The second type is the "prank" variety. Though these houses look safe, with normal lawns and an occasional jack-o'-lantern, they are owned by weirdos or jerks who give out terrible candy or no candy at all. Usually, these houses end up being plastered with rotten eggs or toilet paper by the end of the night. Margie Medford's home is a good example of the "prank" variety.

The third type of house is the "scary" type. These are the houses that look haunted year round, with overgrown lawns, dark porches, no jack-o'-lanterns, and no candy. The only time you visit a spooky home is when someone dares you. The Monger mansion was most definitely of the "scary" variety.

Plenty of these sorts of homes could be found on Anchor

Street. Houses for candy, houses for pranks, and houses for screams. Which made it *the street* in Ashcrumb to visit on Halloween.

Carloads of costumed kids always appeared at sunset, their parents dumping them off on Anchor Street for a night of trick-or-treating. And this Halloween, James Gordon and Hector Figg weren't about to let any moochers beat them to the good candy. So just as the sun began to sink behind the trees, James the gorilla and Hector the vampire set out with their sacks and chaperones in tow.

"Hang out on the sidewalk while we ring the doorbell," James instructed Misty and Yoshi as he and Hector approached their first home. "Hector and I don't want to look like a couple of babies."

Misty and Yoshi nodded, their hands in their pockets. It was cold that evening, cold enough to see one's breath, and it was oddly quiet. No wind was blowing, so the air was very still, so still that smoke from chimneys drifted up in straight lines, like pale gray fingers oozing into the sky.

"Halloween isn't as much fun when you're not in costume," Yoshi said, her teeth chattering a bit.

"I know," said Misty. The girls felt a little out of place, standing on the sidewalk in ordinary clothing. They watched glumly, even a little jealously, as kids rustled past in their costumes. The girls made small talk as they followed James and Hector from house to house, but never did Misty and Yoshi talk about what Misty had seen that morning at the Dearly Departed. There was no need to; they had already discussed it.

In fact, when James told his mother earlier that the girls had been in Misty's room "for hours," he hadn't been kidding. All afternoon the girls had talked about the ghosts Misty had seen through Madame Zaster's glasses and how strangely Mr. Yates had acted. So many questions had popped into their minds. How did Mr. Yates know the riddle from Fannie Belcher's diary? Who was the horrid-looking specter that had appeared in the doublet? What did it all mean?

It was quite a haunted puzzle, a puzzle that Misty didn't feel like figuring out at the moment. All she wanted to do was enjoy Halloween, even if her brother, at the moment, was not.

For, thirty minutes into trick-or-treating, James and Hector made the mistake of paying Margie Medford, the crossing guard, a visit.

"Well, lookee here!" jeered Medford, standing in her doorway, which was already decorated with broken eggs. "It's a monkey and a bloodsucker!"

"I'm a *gorilla*," said James courageously, holding out his bag.

"Here's something for the effort, gorilla-boy," Medford snorted, tossing a handful of loose popcorn—which she'd been munching on when she'd answered the door—into James's bag. "Now scram!"

She cocked her head back, let out a thunderous laugh, and slammed the door so hard that it shook Hector's plastic fangs from his mouth.

"Gross," James groaned, fishing the loose popcorn from his bag.

"Cheer up," Misty told him. "The Sweethouses' home is next."

"Aw, man, check it out!" James yelled to Hector as they scurried up to the Sweethouses' home, where a major candy scene was going on. Crowds of kids surrounded Mrs. Sweethouse, who stood at her front door, reaching into huge boxes of candy and stuffing everyone's sacks. Yoshi and Misty couldn't help wading in on the action.

"Misty!" Mrs. Sweethouse called over the ocean of costumed heads. "I'm so glad you're here. I've got something for you!"

"For *me*?" said Misty.

"Yes, wait right here," said Mrs. Sweethouse. She disappeared into her house and returned momentarily. "Here you go," she said, handing Misty an envelope. Then she whispered in Misty's ear, "It's just a little something that my husband and I wanted to give you. After all you went through the other night with that terrible May Nays, it's the least we could do. Consider it a babysitter bonus!"

Too bashful to open the envelope in front of everyone, Misty thanked Mrs. Sweethouse and pulled Yoshi to the side of the yard.

"Open it!" said Yoshi.

Misty peeked inside the envelope and squealed, "I can't believe it. It's money!"

"Wow!" said Yoshi. "Better keep that away from James!"

"Speaking of James," said Misty, looking for his furry head. "Where did he and Hector go?"

Misty spied little Jimmy Winn, who was dressed as Frankenstein. "Did you happen to see where my brother and Hector Figg went?" she asked him.

"Oh yeah," said Jimmy. "Hector just dared James to go knock on Hazel Monger's door."

"WHAT?" cried Misty.

"Oh great," groaned Yoshi.

The girls took off running in the direction of the Monger mansion, hurrying through the scores of children on the sidewalk, bumping into fairies, and knocking down cowboys.

Finally, they made it to Hazel Monger's iron gate, where Hector stood with a couple of kids, peering inside the mansion's gloomy yard.

"Where's James?" panted Misty.

"Knocking on Hazel Monger's door," answered Hector.

At that moment, Misty heard James yell, "Trick or treat!"

"James!" Misty cried, pushing open the gate. "Come back!"

But it was too late. Hazel Monger had grabbed James and was shaking him furiously.

"Brat!" Hazel snarled, her eyes shining like black marbles in the pale moonlight, as she ripped the mask from James's face.

James wailed as the woman's fingernails dug into his arms. "I was just trick-or-treating. You're hurting me!"

"Let go of him!" yelled Misty, dashing up the steps. By the crazy look in her eyes, Hazel had no intention of letting James go.

"Brat!" the woman screeched again. "Sneaking around, trying to sniff out the secret!" She hunched in on herself, like a cat about to spring. "Know this," she hissed. "I'll die before I tell my precious secret."

"Ha! What secret?" said Misty. "You mean the Golden Three?"

The words flew out of Misty's mouth before she could stop them.

"What did you say?" growled Hazel Monger, turning James loose and glaring at Misty. As James backed down the steps, the woman rustled forward, her head cocked to the side and her mouth hanging open as she rattled her bag of rocks.

"How did you know that?" Hazel shrieked, flinging some rocks at Misty. "Answer me!"

Misty grabbed James, and they all dashed down the street, the icy wind howling in their ears. After a few blocks, they stopped. Misty looked back at the Monger mansion. Hazel had disappeared into the darkness of her dungeon.

"It's okay," Misty said. "Hazel's not following us."

James gulped, his legs shaking so badly that his sack of candy knocked against his knees. He'd never had a scare quite like that.

"Let's call it a night," Yoshi said, taking Hector by the hand. "Come on, I'll walk you home, Hector."

As Hector and Yoshi walked off, Misty put her hands on James's shoulders and looked him in the eye. "Don't breathe a word of this to Mom or Dad," Misty said. "Do you understand?"

"Yes," said James weakly.

James was as good as his word. Back home, he didn't mention a thing about the Hazel Monger incident to his parents. He just hopped onto the couch and started sorting through his candy.

"Misty, honey," said Mrs. Gordon. "I shut your bedroom window. I hope you don't mind. It was freezing in there!"

"My window was open?" said Misty.

"Wide open," said Mrs. Gordon. "And James, I couldn't help noticing what a mess you made in Misty's room. You should have constructed that gorilla costume outside."

"What do you mean?" said James, chewing.

"You left brown fur all over Misty's floor," said Mrs. Gordon.

Misty's heart rose in her throat. She headed to her room and threw open the door.

"Oh no," she said. Her mother had been right; brown fur *was* on the floor, but it wasn't part of James's costume. It was the unmistakable mink of Fannie Belcher's coat, tufts of it on the windowsill and pieces of it on the floor, leading all the way to the desk. Which had an open drawer.

"The diary!" Misty gasped. "It's gone!"

7

The Crystal Ball

How do I look?" Misty said the next afternoon in her room as she modeled her brand-new glasses for Yoshi.

"Much better!" said Yoshi. "See for yourself."

Misty checked her reflection in the vanity's mirror and smiled. Unlike Madame Zaster's glasses—or any of Misty's previous scratched, slipshod pairs—the new frames were sleek and pretty.

"I can actually see your blue eyes!" noticed Yoshi. "So, how did you talk your parents into buying them for you?"

"I didn't," said Misty, biting her lip. "I bought them myself at Optical Illusion Eyeglass Shop just a few hours ago."

"Sly," said Yoshi with a grin.

"I still can't believe how much these glasses cost," admitted Misty. "I spent all the money Mrs. Sweethouse gave me to buy them. Still," she added, "it was worth it, considering I don't have to wear Zaster's creepy cat-eye glasses anymore!"

"Creepy as they are," said Yoshi, "I think you should keep Zaster's glasses with you, like in your bag or something."

"Why?" said Misty.

"Look," said Yoshi seriously. "I know you don't like Zaster's glasses because they allow you to see freaky stuff, but you need to be smart about all this. Until you understand what's going on here, I think you should definitely keep Zaster's glasses with you, just in case. You never know when you might need them."

"Why would I *need* them?" asked Misty.

"In case you need to see *more* than meets the eye," said Yoshi. "With the diary gone, we have no way of knowing what might lay ahead." Yoshi shivered. "There must be some kind of crazy stuff written in that diary for Fannie Belcher's fur coat to break into your room and steal it."

"You're right," said Misty, dropping Madame Zaster's glasses into her bag. "I'll keep them in case I need to see *more* than meets the eye."

Just then, a whirring noise came from outside. Misty and

Yoshi looked out the open window to see a strange-looking silver van pull into the driveway. Atop its roof were small satellite dishes, rotating and making loud electronic beeps.

"That thing looks like a UFO," laughed Yoshi.

"It's Dr. Figg's new van," said Misty. "Hector's been talking about it nonstop."

Suckers for gadgets, Mr. Gordon and James trotted out to the van and began checking it out from front to back. Through the windshield, Dr. Figg and Hector could be seen, adjusting their headsets in the front seat.

Mrs. Gordon joined them at the van and then glanced up at Misty and waved.

"Dr. Figg is going to take us for a ride in his new van!" she called. "He's driving us to see the construction of the new lighthouse. You girls want to come along?"

"No, thanks," said Misty.

"You'll have the house all to yourselves, then," said Mrs. Gordon as everyone climbed in the van. "We'll be back in a little while."

The girls watched the van cruise off, whirring and beeping.

"I'm starving," said Misty. "Let's see if there's anything to eat."

As they headed to the kitchen, they noticed an eerie golden light shining through the crack beneath the door of Mr. Gordon's locked study.

"What's that?" said Yoshi.

"I have no idea," said Misty.

The girls stood in hushed awe as the golden light began to undulate all the way around the edge of the door, framing it in a dazzling shimmer.

"What's going on?" said Misty, spooked, as fingers of mist began pouring through the lock in the doorknob, cascading onto the floor.

And then a phantom voice whispered. "*Missssty Gordon.*"

Recognizing the voice of Madame Zaster's ghost, Misty froze. "Did you hear that?" she asked Yoshi.

"Hear what?" asked Yoshi.

"My name being called."

"I didn't hear anything," said Yoshi, as a fog began rolling down the hall. "Come on, let's get out of here!" she urged, grabbing Misty by the arm.

"*Missssty Gordon,*" the phantom voice spoke again.

Yoshi stopped in her tracks. "I can hear it now," Yoshi said, bewildered. "Now that I'm standing right next to you, I can hear it!"

There was a click, and the study door creaked ajar.

"*Come in,*" the voice beckoned.

Slowly, and a little fearfully, the girls entered the study.

"Look!" said Misty. There stood the séance table, atop which the crystal ball perched, glowing gold. "No wonder I didn't see the séance table at the Dearly Departed. Dad kept it!"

The girls glanced around the hazy room, which looked like a smaller version of the store. Scores of ancient-looking books filled the bookshelves, along with collectable vases and figurines.

They turned and stared in amazement at the crystal ball.

"I've never seen one of those things before," whispered Yoshi.

"Freaky, isn't it?" said Misty, reaching out to touch the orb.

Suddenly, a thin yellow thread of light streaked from the crystal ball and hit Misty's palm with an electrical crackle. In an instant, the light shot back into the ball, and the table trembled.

"What was that?" shouted Misty.

"It's changing colors," said Yoshi, mesmerized, as the orb went from golden yellow to emerald green. The girls sat next to each other at the table and watched as a still image began to appear within the crystal ball, first cloudy, as if in a dream, and then clearer, until coming into focus. And what did the image reveal but a young boy on a bike. He looked very, very familiar to Misty.

"That's my dad!" realized Misty. "That's my dad when he was James's age!"

The girls gazed in wonder at the image.

"I wonder where he's going," said Misty.

Just then, as if granting her request, the image in the crystal ball was set in motion. Misty and Yoshi watched spellbound as the young Mr. Gordon began pedaling down tree-lined Shadow Street.

"The tree tunnel," murmured Misty. What had her dad said on their way to Madame Zaster's house? *I haven't been down this street since I was a boy.*

"I bet he's headed to Madame Zaster's house," said Misty.

Sure enough, young Mr. Gordon stopped his bike in front of Madame Zaster's house, tiptoed to one of its windows, and peeked inside.

"What is he doing?" asked Yoshi.

"He's spying on something going on inside Madame Zaster's house," guessed Misty. "Too bad we can't see what he's looking at. Oh, I wish we could at least *hear* what's going on!"

At that moment, a radio atop Mr. Gordon's desk clicked on by itself. Misty and Yoshi gulped as the thick sound of static came from the radio. They listened intently as the static was replaced by another sound—that of leaves crunching beneath young Mr. Gordon's feet as he moved along the edges of Madame Zaster's house.

"We've got audio!" said Misty.

The girls continued to watch and listen to the crystal ball and the radio as if they were playing a home movie before their eyes. Young Mr. Gordon was getting bold now as he stood outside Madame Zaster's open window, stretching his head higher and higher over the windowsill to get a better view of what was going on inside.

Suddenly, a familiar, hateful voice issued from inside Madame Zaster's cottage: "Someone's spying on us! I'll fix him!"

In the next second, Hazel Monger—younger but still scary—reached out of the window and grabbed young Mr. Gordon.

"Who are you?" she hissed wickedly.

"F-F-Frank Gordon," he stammered, frightened.

"You little brat!" she shrieked, shaking him. "What did you see? What did you hear? Tell me."

"Just something about the Golden Three!" he cried, trying to pull away. "That they're buried somewhere in Ashcrumb!"

She struck him across the face.

"I'm warning you, Frank Gordon," she snarled, her face white with fury. "You better not utter a word of this to anyone! Only the Descendants are the rightful heirs to the Golden Three. Do you understand?"

Frank Gordon whimpered and nodded.

"Forget everything you saw and heard today! And don't you dare . . . ," she added, her black eyes gleaming, "DON'T YOU DARE GET ANY IDEAS!"

Finally, young Mr. Gordon broke from Hazel Monger's grasp, jumped on his bike, and sped off.

The crystal ball glowed violet, and then it went dim, as if a plug had been pulled.

For a minute, Misty and Yoshi just stared at the dark orb.

"That was amazing," said Yoshi.

Misty nodded, awestruck.

"Something just dawned on me," Misty finally said. "Remember the entry in Fannie Belcher's diary? When she was talking about a boy who interrupted the séance?"

"Yeah," said Yoshi.

"Now we know that that boy was my dad!" said Misty. "He got to see all three Descendants at the séance. So far, we know that two of the Descendants were Fannie Belcher and Hazel Monger. I wonder who the third Descendant could be."

"Or rather, *could have been*," added Yoshi. "That person is probably dead by now, like Fannie Belcher."

"What makes you think that the third Descendant is dead?" argued Misty. "After all, hundred-year-old Hazel Monger is still alive, and take Mr. Yates, for example," suggested Misty. "Mr. Yates is ninety-nine and he's still alive and—"

Misty grabbed Yoshi.

"What if . . . ," said Misty.

"What if *what*?" said Yoshi. "Spit it out!"

"What if Mr. Yates is the third Descendant?" said Misty. "Think about it! He's the same age as the other Descendants, and that would explain how he knew Madame Zaster's riddle!"

"Do you really think so?" said Yoshi.

Misty nodded.

"Well, even if Mr. Yates happens to be the third Descendant, we still know nothing about the Golden Three," said Yoshi. "Why don't you just ask your dad about them?"

"Ask my dad?" coughed Misty. "I don't think that's such a good idea. Then he'd know I'd been snooping around. I mean, he'd totally freak if he knew we'd been in his study." Misty got up from the chair. "In fact, let's get out of here right now."

They'd just shut the door behind them when Yoshi paused.

"What happened to your hand?" she asked Misty.

Misty looked. To her surprise, there were mysterious black lines webbing across the palm of her right hand. She quickly rubbed the lines, but they wouldn't come off.

"How weird," said Misty. "I guess I got them from those electrical currents that came out of the crystal ball."

"Do they sting?" asked Yoshi.

"No," said Misty, puzzled.

"Well," said Yoshi, looking at the marks. "Maybe they'll fade away."

But they didn't. In fact, by the end of the day, the marks on Misty's hand had grown as dark and deep as the mystery behind them.

8

The Dark History Lesson

Margie Medford sat in her crossing guard chair, steam rising from her head as she took swigs of piping hot coffee and grumbled to herself. She was in a fouler mood than usual, having had to get up early that morning in order to de-ice the school's crossing lane with salt. Adding to her fury was the fact that the doughnuts she was eating were stale.

She muttered beneath her breath, staring straight ahead at the point where the children would soon appear. What was taking them so long today? She reached into the doughnut box, grabbed the last one, and stuffed it into her mouth. Chewing and brooding, Medford caught sight of some kids headed her way. She tossed the box aside and stood, the ice cracking beneath her. She stretched her arms and waved the STOP sign. She was ready.

"Hurry! Hurry!" she urged a pack of first graders as they struggled in the slush.

A girl in pigtails fell.

"Whiny baby," Medford taunted. "A little ice never hurt anybody!"

Another group trotted past, their heads down like a rushing team of donkeys. "That's right," yelled Medford. "Just keep moving, moving, moving!" She stopped, panting, waiting for the next miserable bunch of weasels.

Medford smiled. Jimmy Winn was coming. She cracked her chapped knuckles and breathed in deeply, her heart racing in anticipation of giving his ears a good boxing.

"There's nothing like thumping ice-cold ears," she chuckled. She was just pulling her arms back when Jimmy came into clearer view. Medford couldn't believe it! The little turkey had worn earmuffs! She stomped her feet and gave him a short, brutish shove. "Chicken!" she bellowed. Oh, what wouldn't she give just to punch a couple of ears this morning!

Medford twitched. Here came Hector Figg, Misty Gordon, and her smarty-pants friend, Yoshi Yamamoto. Medford decided to let them pass. They were too quick, and besides, Medford needed to save up her energy for terrorizing lollygagging James Gordon, who just so happened to be the last kid to lumber across the walk that morning.

Finally, along came James, all by himself, like a lone, defenseless puppy. Medford checked to make sure the coast was clear. It was too good to be true; there wasn't an adult around, not a teacher, not a parent, nobody. James was *all* hers. Medford backed herself behind a tree and waited.

James strode on, but as he passed the tree, he noticed Medford's big brown boots sticking out from behind its trunk like two massive mushrooms. James did a kung fu kick and shot ahead. Medford charged after him, taking a swipe at his ears but missing.

"Arggggh!" she thundered as James made it safely to the other side before disappearing into the castle.

Medford marched back to her chair and kicked the doughnut box. Then she saw something in the trees. A looming, dark figure. Medford took a few steps toward it and squinted. Was that *fur*?

"The p-p-playground beast!" she stammered, frantically bringing the whistle to her mouth and blowing.

◦─────◦

"ATTENTION, FACULTY, STAFF, AND STUDENTS OF ASHCRUMB ELEMENTARY!" Vice Principal Barrel called over the school intercom. "THERE HAS BEEN AN INCIDENT IN FRONT OF THE CASTLE INVOLVING MARGIE MEDFORD. DO NOT PANIC! WE HAVE EVERYTHING UNDER CONTROL."

Misty and Yoshi dashed to their classroom window and looked out at the parking lot, where Margie Medford was being carried away on a stretcher. She was still blowing her whistle as she was loaded into the ambulance.

"Looks like Medford finally blew a fuse," Yoshi said under her breath to Misty.

"That's enough, class," said Mrs. Lane, pulling the blinds down. "Back to your desks."

Standing in front of the chalkboard, Mrs. Lane tucked her messy blonde hair behind her ears and smiled. "I have a special surprise for you, students. As it plays so prominent a role in our town's history, I thought it would be pertinent to discuss the sinking of the *Royal Ashcrumb*.

"Here to explain it is a very special guest, the director of the Ashcrumb Museum, my husband, Mr. Lane!"

The class gave a few feeble claps, and in walked tall, lanky Mr. Lane, decked from head to toe in a dashing seventeenth-century period costume—a broad-brimmed hat, a lace-collared shirt and doublet, breeches, and buckled shoes.

He took a sweeping bow.

"Hear ye! Hear ye!" he said in character. "Listen up as I tell the disastrous story of the sinking of the *Royal Ashcrumb*!"

The class snickered.

"The year was 1630," Mr. Lane began. "It had been ten years since the *Mayflower* had landed in New England. America now had a number of colonies, many of them under the rule of England.

"King Charles I, who happened to be King of England at the time, wanted his very own kingdom in America, a sort of colony just for royalty. It was the King's hope that once this royal colony was established—with castle and all—he would move there.

"The first step toward establishing this new kingdom was swiftly accomplished: King Charles sent the most glorious ship in his fleet, the *Royal Ashcrumb*, to America and founded the Royal Colony of Ashcrumb, which he named after the ship. Within several months, it was peopled with a number of royal colonists.

"The next step, which was to build a castle for His Majesty, took a bit longer. After three years, the castle—which now serves as your school—was finished. The last step was to furnish the castle so that King Charles could move into it. So in 1633 the ship, the *Royal Ashcrumb*, set sail again for the Royal Colony of Ashcrumb with objects for King Charles's new castle.

"But the ship was transporting more than just King Charles's furniture and art!" Mr. Lane paused dramatically, his finger in the air. "The ship was transporting the King's most recently acquired—and prized—possessions: three golden Greek statues of Poseidon, Zeus, and Hades, which were rumored to have magical powers. They had been recently unearthed after being lost for ages."

Misty and Yoshi sat bolt upright and gaped at each other.

"You see, King Charles, who believed in the Divine Right of Kings, felt that these statues, which supposedly had powers over the waters, heavens, and death, would help him achieve absolute rule over everything. With the statues, King Charles truly believed his royal colony in America would become the most powerful kingdom in the world."

Yoshi raised her hand. "Why didn't King Charles just use the statues in England?"

"Historians, such as myself, speculate that His Majesty didn't want to take any chances," replied Mr. Lane. "He probably knew that there were many other parties interested in getting their hands on the statues. Rather than risking the statues being stolen before he could fully understand how to use them, the King decided to ship them off to his new colony, where, in the safety of his controlled kingdom, he could take his time in learning how to harness their powers."

Mr. Lane paused. "Of course, that's just an educated guess," he snorted pompously. "A very, very educated guess, I might add . . . considering I'm a very educated man." He smiled smugly and continued.

"Anyway, where was I? Oh yes! Meanwhile, the county of royal colonists was waiting for the ship to arrive. Finally, one evening, a watchman atop the Bell Tower spotted the *Royal Ashcrumb* and rang the bell, signaling the arrival of the ship to the other colonists. Alas, it would be the last time the bell would ring, for it would soon be damaged in the foul weather that was brewing.

"For an Atlantic Skull-a-Buster, the most wicked of sea storms, came out of nowhere. As the ship sailed into the bay, it was struck by lightning and caught on fire. It quickly began to sink.

"The fire and raging storm consumed nearly everyone aboard the ship. As for the three golden statues, they were lost.

"With his precious statues gone, King Charles's hopes for supreme rule were dashed, and he abandoned his dream of a royal colony, not even making the overseas journey to visit his new castle. And some years later," added Mr. Lane, removing his hat and placing it over his belly, "His Highness was beheaded. . . . And that is the story of the *Royal Ashcrumb*. Are there any questions?"

"So, who were the survivors?" asked Misty.

"Sadly, only three passengers of the *Royal Ashcrumb* survived the disaster," said Mr. Lane. "They were among the *Royal Ashcrumb*'s crew: Captain Nicholas Yates and his officers, William Monger and Benton Belcher.

"Interestingly," added Mr. Lane, "until recently, the last three descendants of Captain Yates and Officers Belcher and Monger could be found—still alive—in town. With the passing of the late Fannie Belcher, the final two are Hazel Monger and Mr. Louis Yates."

"Louis Yates works at my dad's antique store," said Misty.

Mr. Lane gave Misty a curious look.

The bell rang, and the students began to file out of the room.

"Excuse me," said Mr. Lane, stopping Misty on her way out. "Could I speak with you for a moment?"

"Sure."

"Did you say that you know Mr. Louis Yates?"

"Yes," replied Misty. "Like I said, he works at my family's antique store."

"Well, the truth is, the Ashcrumb Museum has been trying for years to persuade Mr. Yates to let us buy a particular item that he has in his possession." Mr. Lane rubbed his hands together. "I really believe that the museum should have this item, since it is such an historic piece."

"What is it?" asked Misty.

"It's a doublet," said Mr. Lane. "An old, black doublet from the sixteen hundreds. Do you know the one I'm talking about?"

"Yes," said Misty. "Mr. Yates offered to let my brother wear it as a Halloween costume."

"WHAT?" cried Mr. Lane, shocked. "Mr. Yates was going to let a *boy* wear an important historic artifact for trick-or-treating? I'm appalled!"

"Why?" asked Misty. "What's the big deal?"

"I'll tell you what the big deal is," said Mr. Lane, becoming more irritated by the minute. "That doublet happened to belong to Captain Yates! It was the very doublet that the revered Captain Yates was wearing when the *Royal Ashcrumb* sank! It was handed down to Louis Yates as an heirloom, of course."

"Are you sure it belonged to Captain Yates?" said Misty, recalling the grisly apparition that had appeared wearing the doublet.

"Yes, I'm sure!" snorted Mr. Lane, indignant. "I'm an expert! I happen to be the director of the Ashcrumb Museum for a reason, you know."

Misty wondered. How could the bloody, horrifying ghost she saw in the doublet at the Dearly Departed have been the spirit of Captain Yates? The evil-looking spirit had hardly looked like a revered royal captain.

Suddenly, Misty remembered the skull-and-snake tattoo on the ghost's neck and the words, *Black Adders*.

"Are you certain that the doublet didn't belong to a man named Black Adders?" asked Misty.

"Black Adders?" choked Mr. Lane. "Of course not! The Black Adders was the name of a gang of pirates. Clever pirates, too. Very diabolical. They called themselves the Black Adders because they were like snakes that would slip into other people's skins. They were always disguising themselves. They would take over ships, kill everyone aboard, and then assume the identity of their victims.

"But enough of the Black Adders!" barked Mr. Lane, flustered. "Would you please try to convince Mr. Yates to sell the doublet to the museum? It's bad enough that Ashcrumb Elementary uses the *Royal Ashcrumb*'s mermaid figurehead as playground equipment! And now Mr. Yates is turning another one of its precious artifacts into a Halloween costume!"

Mr. Lane was growing redder by the moment. "Will you please talk to Mr. Yates about the doublet?"

"Okay," Misty murmured.

"Thank you," said Mr. Lane, regaining his composure. "You know, you look a little pale. You might be coming down with a cold."

"Mr. Lane," said Misty weakly.

"Yes?"

"What became of the Black Adders?"

"Nobody knows," he replied, checking his watch. "They disappeared about the same time the *Royal Ashcrumb* sank. Well, I suppose you should be off to your next class." He tipped his hat at Misty. "I hope you've learned some interesting tidbits about Ashcrumb's history." Then he walked off, his buckled shoes clattering down the hall.

Tidbits? How about this for a tidbit, Mr. Lane, thought Misty. *It may have been Captain Yates and his crew who set sail from England to America, but it wasn't they who steered the* Royal Ashcrumb *into Ashcrumb Bay. It was the gang of pirates, the Black Adders, disguised as Captain Yates, Officer Monger, Officer Belcher, and crew.*

Which could only mean that the *Royal Ashcrumb* had been taken over at sea by pirates. And why would pirates have seized the ship? Could it be they knew the golden Greek statues of Zeus, Poseidon, and Hades were on board and believed they possessed powers?

That would explain the beginning of the riddle:

When English garb did fool the county,
Snakes passed in with royal bounty . . .

"The 'Snakes' were the Black Adders," Misty whispered to herself, "and the 'royal bounty' was the golden statues."

Misty walked down the hall as if in a daze, bumping into people as she thought about it all. Not only had Misty learned what the Golden Three were, she had discovered what "Descendants" meant—descendants of the Black Adders. The last three remaining Descendants were the late Fannie Belcher, Hazel Monger, and Mr. Yates, who believed they were the rightful heirs to the mythical and powerful Golden Three, magic treasures that had yet to be found.

Misty stood at her locker, chills running down her spine. Strangely, she now found herself gripped by the mystery that had driven and haunted the Descendants . . .

Were the Golden Three buried in Ashcrumb? And if so . . . where?

Yoshi approached. "What's the matter, Misty?" she asked. "You look completely weirded out! Tell me what Mr. Lane said to you back there."

"Okay," whispered Misty. "But be prepared to be weirded out, too."

But nothing could have prepared Yoshi for what she was about to hear.

9

The Very-Long-Distance Phone Call

Breakfast as usual, Mr. Gordon was scanning the obituaries in the Saturday newspaper.

"So, did anybody interesting bite the dust?" James asked his father.

"James!" Mrs. Gordon fussed, shaking her head. "Mind your manners. Don't say 'bite the dust.'"

"Okay, then," said James, rolling his eyes. "Did anybody interesting *buy the farm*?"

"No," said Mr. Gordon. "Nobody interesting bit the dust, bought the farm, or kicked the bucket."

"That's too bad," said James, smearing jelly on his toast.

"Ah, listen to this," said Mr. Gordon, tapping the paper.

"Evidently, the Ashcrumb Museum is restoring the legendary Ashcrumb Bell. Mr. Lane, the director of the museum, says here that the museum is lowering the bell today in order to repair it. The bell will be up and ringing in a couple of weeks."

"Well, I've got some way cooler news, much cooler than that ugly old bell," said James. "Dr. Figg told me that the Ashcrumb Lighthouse is going to be finished ahead of schedule. It's going to be amazing, man."

"That's something," chirped Mrs. Gordon. Then she looked at Misty and tilted her head. "You look different, dear," she said. "Did you do something to your hair?"

"I got new glasses," said Misty.

"*New* glasses?" sputtered Mr. Gordon, dropping his fork.

"Don't worry, Dad," said Misty. "Mrs. Sweethouse gave me a babysitter bonus, and it was enough money for the glasses."

"Whew," said Mr. Gordon, relieved. "I didn't mean to get stirred up. It's just that, well . . . business has been slow lately."

"I'm sure business will pick up," Mrs. Gordon said.

"Yeah," added James. "Before you know it, somebody will take a dirt nap!"

"That's the spirit!" chuckled Mr. Gordon, patting James on the head.

There was a knock at the door. Eager to leave the kitchen table, Misty yelled, "I got it!"

It was Yoshi. "Am I interrupting anything?" she asked.

"No, not at all," said Misty. "Just the basic crazy morning stuff." She looked at a paper sack Yoshi was holding. "What's that?" she asked.

"It's my dad's lunch," said Yoshi. "He forgot it, so I'm going to take it to him. Do you want to walk with me?"

"To the asylum?" said Misty, wincing. Then she shrugged her shoulders. "Oh, why not? It couldn't be any more crazy than it is here."

Misty reached for her coat.

"Oh wow," whispered Yoshi. "Look at your hand."

"Shhh," said Misty, grabbing her bag. "We'll talk about it outside." Then Misty called toward the kitchen, "Yoshi and I are going for a walk. Be back in a little while!"

As soon as the girls were on the sidewalk, Yoshi took Misty's right hand and turned it palm up. "That is so freaky! It looks like a tattoo." Yoshi squinted at the thick black lines that had gotten even darker.

"I know," said Misty. "I've tried washing it off, but nothing has worked."

The girls braced against an icy wind.

"It's freezing out here," said Misty, taking her gloves from her bag and slipping them on.

"Yeah, come on," suggested Yoshi. "Let's start walking."

Ashcrumb rarely looked pleasant at that dreary time of year, and today was no exception. The cold, hard look of November, with its gray skies and frostbitten grass, had even made the Sweethouses' cheerful home seem dismal. One could imagine how completely forbidding the Monger mansion looked that morning.

As they passed the mansion's iron gate, the girls stole a glance at its dark and empty front porch.

"Witch Hazel must be inside today," Yoshi guessed.

Another biting Atlantic gust blew against the girls, sending leaves swirling past them and high-pitched howls whistling across rooftops. Over their heads, a seagull fluttered and swooped in the wind.

Misty stopped walking for a moment. "Do you hear that noise?"

"Which one?" said Yoshi.

"That rustling sound," replied Misty, looking about curiously.

"It's probably just leaves," said Yoshi. "Come on, let's keep walking."

By the time they reached the asylum's gate, a light fog had arisen. Yoshi pushed a button on the gate, and the girls waited a moment before a voice came through a speaker.

"State your business, please."

"Hi, it's Yoshiko Yamamoto," Yoshi called into the speaker. "I'm here to see my dad."

"Hello, Miss Yamamoto," said the voice. "Your father is expecting you."

The gate buzzed open, and the girls walked through.

Misty looked over the vast grounds. There were only a few people outside, mostly nurses taking coffee breaks on benches. One nurse got up and walked toward the girls.

"Hi, Yoshi, are you here to see your father?" she asked.

"Yes," said Yoshi, holding up the sack. "I brought his lunch."

"Why don't you just leave that with me?" said the nurse a bit nervously. "You see, Dr. Yamamoto is tied up at the moment and won't be able to visit with you."

"Why?" asked Yoshi. "What is he doing?"

"He's trying to get a grip on a new patient," whispered the nurse. "She's quite a handful."

Suddenly, a whistle shrieked from a cluster of trees. Everyone spun around.

"It's Margie Medford!" gasped Misty as the crossing guard jumped out from the trees and blew again on her whistle, motioning for some nurses to walk past.

Dr. Yamamoto, who was nearly two feet shorter than the giant Medford, was hopping up and down, trying to swipe the whistle from her mouth.

"Evidently," the nurse explained in a confidential tone, "Miss Medford has not taken that whistle out of her mouth since she saw—or rather, *imagined* that she saw—the alleged playground beast at Ashcrumb Elementary."

"She saw it?" both girls exclaimed together.

The nurse nodded. "Imagined or not, the sighting sent her right over the edge."

"So *that* was the 'incident' that happened in front of the castle involving Medford," said Yoshi.

"Be quiet!" yelled Dr. Yamamoto, covering his ears as Medford blasted away on the whistle. At his wit's end, Dr. Yamamoto suddenly broke into Japanese, shouting, "*Shizukani shiro!*"

"What did he say?" Misty asked Yoshi.

"He said 'be quiet' in Japanese," translated Yoshi.

Dr. Yamamoto spotted Yoshi and waved. Medford looked. Immediately, the crossing guard stopped blowing on her whistle and squinted at the girls.

"Medford sees us," Misty told the nurse. "What is she going to do?"

"There's no telling," warned the nurse.

Medford remained motionless, except for a twitching eye. Dr. Yamamoto slowly lowered his hands from his ears and scribbled in a notepad.

"I think we should be going, Yoshi," said Misty. "Your dad is obviously very busy."

They walked back out the gate and had just stepped onto

the sidewalk when Medford charged the closed gate, blowing frantically on the whistle and pointing across the street, past the girls, toward a hazy grove of sycamores. Medford spit out the whistle and blurted, "THERE IT IS AGAIN! THE PLAYGROUND BEAST!"

Everyone turned to look but saw nothing.

Dr. Yamamoto and the nurses took Medford by the arms, but the crossing guard could not be calmed.

"Yoshiko, Misty," Dr. Yamamoto called through the fence as he and the nurses led Medford back to the facility. "Another time."

Yoshi waved good-bye to her dad and started down the street, but not Misty. She wanted to see if Medford was indeed imagining things. Misty looked across the street to where Medford had just been pointing. At first, Misty saw only the fog among the trees. Then, from behind a sycamore, out crept Fannie Belcher's coat. It swayed menacingly, its fur rippling in the wind.

Misty swallowed, going weak in the knees as she reached into her bag and pulled out Madame Zaster's glasses. Trembling, she took off her own glasses and put on Madame Zaster's. They turned icy cold and fogged over.

"No way," whispered Misty.

There, standing in the fur coat, was the ghost of Fannie

Belcher. She was a smoky gray color, her eyes pale silver and her mouth a dark hole. The ghost leaned forward sinisterly. "*Misty Gordon*," the frightful apparition called, its eyes flickering. "*You listen here . . .*" But Misty didn't hang around to hear what the ghost had to say.

"I can't believe it!" Yoshi cried when they were back in Misty's room. "I can't believe that you didn't stay to hear what Fannie Belcher's ghost had to say!"

"Why should I?" said Misty, peering leerily out her bedroom window. "She was so scary-looking!"

"Scary-looking or not," said Yoshi, "she wanted to tell you something. It was probably something really important, and you ran away."

Misty considered that maybe she *had* acted hastily in running away from the ghost.

"Okay," sighed Misty. "I promise the next time that Fannie Belcher's ghost tries to say something I'll be brave and listen."

Just then, a loud, buzzing ring filled the room. The girls jumped as Fannie Belcher's phone sounded. And there was no doubt about it—the phone was definitely ringing this time! *Answer me, answer me*, it seemed to clang, inching along the desktop like a terrible black bug.

Bewildered, Misty reached for the phone and then paused,

her hand hovering above the receiver. She closed her eyes. She couldn't bear answering it. As if the phone could sense her reluctance, its receiver shot upward, landing in the palm of Misty's hand as soundly as a hurled baseball.

Her arm quivering, she brought the phone to her ear.

"Hello?" she said.

For a few seconds, all Misty heard on the line was static. Then came a softer noise, like the sound of the ocean when you hold a seashell to your ear. Over that ocean traveled a voice, at first faraway, as if calling from a distant cliff, and then the voice drew closer and clearer, until breaking through all at once: *This is the operator. There is a Fannie Belcher on the line. Would you like to accept the call?*

One lesson horror movies teach is that you should never invite a ghoul into your home. No matter how much a ghoul pleads, you never let him slip one dark, skinny, hungry foot through your doorway. Because you know that once you give him permission to step inside your house, you're doomed.

Holding the phone in her hand, Misty couldn't help but wonder what she might be inviting into her *life* by accepting this call. The choice was up to her. She could either slam the phone down or she could simply say:

"Yes."

Thank you, said the operator. *Hold for Fannie Belcher.*

It was completely creepy, waiting on the line for a ghost, and it was even creepier when the ghost finally spoke.

"Hello . . . Misty Gordon."

The voice was hollow and strange, as if it were speaking from the bottom of a well.

"I'm here," answered Misty, pulling Yoshi to her side so she could listen in on the conversation.

"Since you wouldn't speak to me on the street, I decided to reach you by phone," the ghost said, a cutting tone in its voice.

"What do you want?" said Misty.

"I want you to mind your own business," the ghost warned. "My diary and its contents are none of your affair. Be warned! Do not interfere with the prophecy!"

"What prophecy?" asked Misty.

"The prophecy found in the riddle," hissed the ghost. "Oh, I've been watching you . . . and I know you're trying to figure it all out."

The phone line crackled, and Fannie Belcher's voice began to fade in and out.

"You're just like your father," said the ghost. "Sticking your nose in places it doesn't belong! Frank Gordon," she growled, speaking his name as if it were something unsavory, "with his ridiculous store. Well, that store of his never fooled me!"

"What are you talking about?" asked Misty.

"Years ago, when your father was a boy and eavesdropped on the séance at Madame Zaster's house and learned that the Golden Three were somewhere in Ashcrumb, we Descendants knew he wouldn't let it out of his mind. And we were right! He grew up and started his business—the Dearly Departed—that allowed him to go through dead people's things in hopes of uncovering clues to where the Golden Three might be.

"We Descendants were guarded. We knew that the Dearly Departed was just a front. But then Louis Yates, that mindless sop Louis Yates, started to go soft in the head. He forgot that he was a Descendant. And that vulture Gordon, knowing that Yates was a link to the Golden Three, hired him to work at the store. Hazel and I knew what your father was up to: He was hoping that Yates might unthinkingly offer some clue, some key in finding the Golden Three."

Misty's head began to swim.

"So you listen to me, Misty Gordon," said the ghost. "You may have learned the prophecy from my diary before I got it back, but that's all you're going to learn!"

Misty interrupted. "Why do you even care about the Golden Three? You're dead, after all!"

The ghost gave a low, self-satisfied laugh. "The statue of Hades can bring the dead back to life. Once the Snakes' spirits find the statues, they will honor their descendants by bringing us back from the dead! And when that occurs—and if you have at all interfered with the prophecy—I promise that the *first* thing I will do is . . . *kill and devour Misty Gordon.*"

The ghost let out a bone-chilling laugh, and then the line went dead.

And Misty, having watched plenty of horror movies, realized that she hadn't learned any lessons from them. With a simple yes, she had let something in after all.

10

The Hypno-Clock

Misty hung up the phone and looked at Yoshi.

"I knew I shouldn't have answered that phone," said Misty. "Now I'm really in deep trouble!"

"Yeah," agreed Yoshi. "Fannie Belcher has really got it in for you. Not to mention Hazel Monger."

"Wow, thanks for making me feel better," said Misty sarcastically.

Yoshi plopped down on the bed. "But until the Ashcrumb Bell rings, I wouldn't get too worried about it. After all, the fulfilling of the prophecy all depends on the Ashcrumb Bell ringing, right? And, as we all know, that broken old bell will probably never gong again."

Misty jumped. "I just remembered something! The news-paper mentioned that the Ashcrumb Museum is lowering the Ashcrumb Bell today to repair it. It will be up and ringing in a couple of weeks."

"That is *so* not good," said Yoshi. "That means we don't have much time to find the Golden Three."

"How are we supposed to find the Golden Three when the Descendants haven't been able to find them themselves?" Misty said in frustration. "And according to Belcher's ghost, my father has spent most of his life looking for the Golden Three, and he's come up empty-handed as well."

"So you do believe what Fannie Belcher's ghost said, that your father has been trying to find the Golden Three ever since he overheard the séance as a boy?" asked Yoshi.

"Yes," said Misty. "For as long as I can remember, my dad has always seemed to be searching for things . . . and not just for things to sell in the store, either. I mean, whenever he rummages through dead people's stuff, he gets this weird look on his face, like he's on a strange mission."

"Well, why don't you just tell your father everything you know?" asked Yoshi.

"Are you kidding?" said Misty. "It's obvious by his locked study that this is his secret. If he learned that I'm involved in something so dangerous as trying to find the Golden Three, he'd flip out."

The girls sat on the bed for a while, deep in thought.

"I've got an idea," Yoshi said, twirling her black ponytail around her finger.

"What?"

"I think we should do some snooping around Mr. Yates's room at the Dearly Departed," suggested Yoshi. "We might find something that he's forgotten about. Like Fannie Belcher just let slip . . . 'some clue, some key in finding the Golden Three.'"

Key . . . Misty thought to herself, pondering the two keys Mr. Yates wore on a necklace. She knew that one key was for his bedroom, but she had no idea what the other one—an old skeleton key—was for. Misty had even asked Mr. Yates on several occasions what the old key unlocked, to which Mr. Yates had given his usual reply: "Don't recall . . . don't recall."

Misty reflected on the way Mr. Yates had instinctively clutched his necklace for a brief moment that morning in the Dearly Departed, right after he'd spoken part of the riddle. Was there a link between whatever the skeleton key unlocked and the prophecy?

"You're right," Misty said. "We should snoop around Mr. Yates's room. But in order to get into his room, we need to sneak the keys from his necklace." Misty crossed her arms. "Which means we'll have to do it while he's asleep."

"But what if he's not asleep?" asked Yoshi.

"Then we'll *put* him to sleep," said Misty, a glint of mischief in her eyes.

"How?" said Yoshi, puzzled.

"Leave that to me," said Misty, grinning.

⌒

"Welcome to the Dearly Departed!" Mr. Yates cried from a chair.

"It's just me," said Misty as she and Yoshi entered the store. "You don't have to get up, Mr. Yates."

"Oh," he said, drowsily. "A young Gordon. What brings you and your friend to the store?"

"We found an old pocket watch," said Misty, "and we thought you could tell us if it's worth something."

"Pocket watch, ay?" said Mr. Yates, sitting up. "Well, let me have a look at it. Come . . . sit here," he said, patting a dilapidated couch next to his chair.

The girls took a seat. Misty opened her bag and pulled out Madame Zaster's Hypno-Clock. Holding its gold chain, Misty let the timepiece slide slowly out of her hand, and with a subtle movement, she set the captivating gold watch swaying back and forth in front of Mr. Yates's face.

"How interesting," he said, his eyes dazzled.

"It is . . . isn't it?" said Misty in a hushed voice.

Mr. Yates nodded, his eyes following the Hypno-Clock as it

swung to and fro like a pendulum. As he settled into the rhythm of the clock's swaying, Misty read in a low voice the engraving on the back of the timepiece:

> *"Listen to the tick, and listen to the tock,*
> *You're growing ever-sleepy from the swaying*
> *Hypno-Clock."*

Misty repeated the verse, and Mr. Yates's eyelids began to droop.

"What . . . an . . . amazing . . . timepiece," he yawned.

With every tick and with every tock, Mr. Yates's eyes grew heavier and heavier, until they shut altogether. His head bobbing, he let out a snort and then fell back against the chair in a deep sleep.

"It worked," whispered Yoshi in awe.

Misty smiled. "Now for the keys."

Carefully, Misty lifted the necklace over Mr. Yates's snoring head.

Keys in hand, Misty motioned for Yoshi to follow her. Quietly, the girls crept catlike down the hall to Mr. Yates's bedroom door, unlocked it with the ordinary key, and went inside.

Mr. Yates's room was small and surprisingly tidy. Against one wall stood a mahogany four-poster bed, covered in a faded but elegant emerald green quilt. Upon his bedside table was a lighted Tiffany lamp and a pair of spectacles. Opposite the bed was a fireplace with a mantelpiece of carved marble.

Misty and Yoshi scanned the room, looking for something with a lock upon it that the skeleton key might fit.

"This key has got to be for *something*," Misty said. "I have a feeling that whatever it unlocks is in this room. *But where*?"

At that moment, they heard a strange noise that sounded as if a small object was rolling across the floor. But nothing was there. At least, it *seemed* as though nothing was there.

This called for Madame Zaster's glasses. Misty put them on and took a deep breath as an icy haze frosted the lenses.

"Wait a second," said Misty. "I see somebody."

The "somebody" happened to be the same ghost of the little boy she'd seen playing marbles during her last visit to the store. Dressed in knickers and a cap, the translucent boy was crouched in the middle of the room, rolling a marble across the floor. Misty watched as, with a light clank, the marble dropped into a tiny hole in one of the wooden planks.

"Bull's-eye!" the boy said, pleased. Then he grabbed up his bag of marbles, turned around, and walked straight through the door.

Misty looked curiously at the hole. She dropped to her knees and stuck her finger into the opening. "The floor is hollow," she said. She jiggled the plank and lifted it, revealing a compartment beneath the floor.

"There's something down there," said Yoshi, peering into the dark space. "It looks like an old wooden box."

"Let me see if I can get it out," said Misty, sticking her hands into the tight space. "I've got it."

The smell of dank earth rose into the air as Misty lifted out the box and set it on the floor. Judging by the thick layer of dirt atop it, the box had been resting, undisturbed, in its hiding place for a very long time.

Misty blew the debris from it and smiled.

"I think we've just discovered what the skeleton key is for," she said, tapping on the lock of the box.

As she'd guessed, the skeleton key was a perfect fit. The lid opened with a creak.

Inside were dusty bundles of yellowed parchment paper, rolled scroll-like and wrapped with twine. Misty took one out and untied it. Carefully, she unfurled it against the floor.

"Wow," said Misty. "What a *map*!"

Indeed. An old, decorative sea chart of the North Atlantic, the map showed the eastern edge of America and the western coast of England and the great expanse of ocean between them. Though tattered and worn, the hand-painted chart, replete with lush ornamentation, still glowed with radiant color.

"It's so beautiful!" said Yoshi. "And look," she added, pointing to a tiny painting of a ship moored at England's shores and then reading the inscription below it. "It's the *Royal Ashcrumb!*"

As Yoshi gazed at the little ship, Misty's eyes drifted to the crumpled, bottom-right corner of the parchment, where an elaborate oval contained the title and date of the map.

"Oh my gosh!" Misty squealed. "This is Captain Yates's sea chart! It's the very map he used on the *Royal Ashcrumb* to sail over here!"

"How do you know?" said Yoshi.

"It says so right here," said Misty, tapping on the oval.

Scooting over, Yoshi read aloud the hazy script: "*Voyage of His Majesty's Ship the* Royal Ashcrumb, *under the command of Captain Nicholas Yates, 1630.*"

Misty scrambled for another scroll and unfurled it. It was another map. Emblazoned in black across its top were the words *The Royal Colony of Ashcrumb, 1633.*

"This is the map of our town!" said Misty. "And even though this map is hundreds of years old, the town hasn't changed much since the map was made."

It was true. Though more roads had been added since 1633, the original roads in Ashcrumb—Plunder Street, Anchor Street, and Shadow Street—were clearly marked in three thick, wandering lines on the map. Ashcrumb Castle and the Bell

Tower, the two main structures that existed at the time, were also depicted by little paintings.

Misty stared spellbound at the old town map. There was something very eerie about the wobbly, thick configuration of the roads.

Yoshi unfurled another scroll.

"Take a look at this," Yoshi declared.

Upon the parchment was a painting of Poseidon, the Greek god believed to have power over the sea. In his hand, he held a trident.

"He's standing on a pedestal, as if he's a statue," noted Misty. "This must be a painting of one of the Golden Three!"

Below the painting a short message was scrawled:

To summon the force of mighty Poseidon,
Look to the points of his golden trident.
Aim them well upon the sea,
And command, "Poseidon, pass your power through me."

"What does that mean?" wondered Yoshi.

"I think it's directions on how to use the statue," guessed Misty.

"So it's like . . . an owner's manual?" mused Yoshi.

"Exactly."

Misty opened the two remaining scrolls. Each had a painting of one of the Golden Three. There was Zeus, believed to have power over the heavens. In his hand, he held a lightning bolt. The other painting was of Hades, the darkest god of all. Hades was believed to have power over the underworld, the dead. Both Zeus and Hades had a similar, brief message scrawled beneath them.

"How frustrating," said Yoshi. "Here are the instructions on how to use the Golden Three, but without the actual statues, the instructions are worthless. To make matters worse, there's no way to find the statues! I mean, these maps don't even have an *X* like pirate maps ought to have!"

"I know," said Misty. "That *is* weird. There is no mark anywhere on this map that even *hints* at the location of the Golden Three."

Suddenly, the bells at the store entrance jingled.

"Someone just came in," Misty whispered frantically. "Quick! Give me the scrolls!"

In a blink, Misty shoved the scrolls into her bag, while Yoshi replaced the empty box and the plank. Out of the room they rushed, shutting the door behind them.

"Hello!" came a voice from the very front of the store.

Misty and Yoshi shot down the hall and skidded next to Mr. Yates, who was just snorting awake. Misty dropped the necklace back over his head, just in time for Mr. Yates to cry, "Welcome to the Dearly Departed!"

"Just looking," said the tourist, his camera swinging below his neck.

"Well, by all means, do look around," said Mr. Yates, getting up from the chair as he recited his usual sales pitch. "There's plenty to look at and much to find at the Dearly Departed. If you dig deep enough, you're certain to find something. Isn't that right, young Gordon?"

"Absolutely," said Misty, patting her bag that contained the scrolls. "Absolutely."

11

The Solitary Gong

Leaving the Dearly Departed, Misty and Yoshi were nearly blown off their feet by a gust of wind tearing down the street.

"Hang on to yer hats!" Sam Port called to the girls from the doorway of the Hum Rum Tavern. "The winds are gettin' wicked!" He touched Misty on the elbow and added emphatically, "I wouldn't walk in that direction, if I were you."

"Why?" asked Misty.

"They're having trouble with the ole Ashcrumb Bell," Mr. Port shouted over the whistling gales. "A crew was lowering the bell from the tower when the winds picked up. They halted the job when most of the ropes holding the bell snapped in two.

Right now, it's dangling by one rope, and who knows how long it'll hold . . . seeing that these winds are gettin' stronger." Mr. Port nodded grimly. "I wager that that ole bell is gonna fall, and you don't want to be standing under it when *that* happens!"

The girls ran down the street to see the spectacle.

"Stand back, stand back," a police officer ordered Misty and Yoshi as they reached the base of the Bell Tower, where a crowd had gathered.

The girls looked up and gasped.

Fifty feet in the air, leaning against the side of the tower, was the massive Ashcrumb Bell, hanging in place by one thin rope. Fluttering in the wind like streamers were the other ropes that had given way.

A group of firefighters stared up at the bell, shaking their heads. "Doesn't look good," Misty overheard one saying.

A sickening *CREAK* sounded. Everyone grew quiet and gazed at the bell. The creaking grew louder as the rope stretched, sending the bell inching downward, scraping against the tower as it went.

"She's about to drop!" shouted a firefighter. "Everybody back up!"

And with a noise that sounded like a tree branch breaking, the rope snapped.

Screams filled the air as the huge and heavy bell broke

loose and fell, shooting down the side of the tower, its insides humming low and terrible, before landing with a ground-shaking, deafening . . .

. . . and *solitary GONG.*

There was somebody new blowing on the school crossing-guard whistle Monday morning. It was Coach Knuckles, and he was enjoying it immensely.

"Look, he thinks he's a cop," snickered James as Misty, Yoshi, and he joined a large group of students waiting to cross the street.

Coach Knuckles blew two short toots, jerked his head, and gestured stiffly with his hands, but no one understood what he meant by his signaling. All the students knew was that you crossed when Medford *chased* you, and you ran when she *hit* you.

Jimmy Winn darted across the street, but nobody followed his lead. The puzzled group was frozen in place, reluctant as a herd of cows having to cross a river.

The coach rolled his eyes.

"Let's hustle!" he shouted at the students. "Look alive, Gordon!" he added, blowing the whistle shrilly in Misty's ear before barking at her like a drill sergeant. "Pick up those feet! That's right! That's more like it, Gordon!"

Misty turned red and gulped.

Unfortunately, Coach Knuckles wasn't the only nasty surprise Misty would have that morning.

"We're having a test?" cried Misty, goggle-eyed as Mrs. Hale passed a math test around.

"Did you forget?" said Mrs. Hale, pausing at Misty's desk.

Misty nodded sheepishly. Mrs. Hale frowned and crossed her arms. "Misty Gordon, don't tell me that you were so busy during the weekend that you couldn't study for a math test!"

Misty's heart sank as she gazed at the test. A full sheet of equations! She gave a sideways glance at Yoshi, math-whiz extraordinaire, who was already burning the lead as she hashed out the answers. Mrs. Hale stood at the front of the room, stopwatch in hand as she timed Yoshi. It was no secret that Mrs. Hale was grooming Yoshi Yamamoto for mathematical greatness.

Misty, however, was grooming herself for mathematical doom. What few formulas she did know seemed to fly out of her head. Listening to everyone scribble and erase only made matters worse.

Yoshi slammed her pencil down. Mrs. Hale clicked the stopwatch and gave Yoshi a proud smile and thumbs-up.

"How did you do?" Yoshi asked Misty after class.

"Don't ask," sighed Misty as they moved down the hall. "My parents are going to kill me."

Mrs. Lane greeted the class with reddened eyes. She looked completely frazzled. She wiped at her face and blew her nose loudly into a handkerchief as she waited for the students to take their seats.

"Pardon me," she sniffed. Everyone gave each other puzzled looks as Mrs. Lane dabbed at her eyes and bit her lip. A quiet, awkward minute passed, in which the squeak of the custodian's cart could be heard in the hallway.

"It's just that my husband called a few minutes ago from the Ashcrumb Museum. As if the falling of the Ashcrumb Bell weren't bad enough, it seems that the museum was robbed over the weekend. Every artifact from the *Royal Ashcrumb* was stolen. It's all gone!" She waved her handkerchief in the air. "Ship rigging, cannons, the three-ton anchor! Even more unbelievable," she added, "the thieves even took the sunken hull of the ship itself!"

"How could that even be possible?" asked Alexis Lenox. "How could someone raise a sunken ship without anybody knowing about it?"

"I don't know!" cried Mrs. Lane. "It's as if it all just . . . *disappeared*."

In no condition to teach, Mrs. Lane instructed the class to read from their textbooks, a task which was nearly imposs-ible, considering the noises Mrs. Lane was making in her handkerchief.

Finally, the bell rang for recess.

"What do you think *that* was all about?" Yoshi said to Misty as they strolled outside.

"You mean you haven't guessed?" said Misty. "Now that the Ashcrumb Bell has tolled, the prophecy is unfolding. The artifacts and the ship weren't stolen. They were *reclaimed* by the spirits of the Snakes!"

Yoshi shivered. "They're headed back to town on the *Royal Ashcrumb*!"

"That's right," said Misty grimly.

Suddenly, some first graders began shrieking and crying.

"What's going on?" said Yoshi as teachers dashed past.

"Oh my!" screamed Mrs. Lane.

"CALL THE POLICE!" ordered Mr. Barrel.

Misty and Yoshi shoved their way through the horde of students that had gathered around a huge hole. The hole that had once contained the *Royal Ashcrumb*'s figurehead.

"The mermaid is gone!" wailed Mrs. Lane.

Misty and Yoshi stared, flabbergasted, into the gaping black opening in the ground.

Mrs. Lane yanked out her handkerchief again. "Well," she said, "I just hope that the thieves who stole the mermaid put her to good use!"

Don't worry, thought Misty. *They will.*

The evening news was filled with stories of "The *Royal Ashcrumb* Robberies." Mr. Gordon, Misty, Yoshi, and James sat transfixed in front of the television, its volume cranked to an eardrum-splitting level as a reporter gave the lowdown on the mysterious occurrence.

"Police are at a total loss," said the newscaster, "as to how the historic pieces were actually stolen. After going over security tapes, there is no evidence of breaking and entering. From the three-ton anchor to the actual sunken hull of the famous ship, everything simply vanished."

Mr. Gordon turned off the TV. With a pensive look on his face, he quietly crossed to the fireplace and poked at the glowing coals.

"I just don't understand it," said Mrs. Gordon, standing in the doorway of the kitchen. "Why would anyone steal the stuff of an old ship? And to go to the lengths of raising that sunken vessel out of the ocean?"

"Yeah, man," said James from the depths of the couch. "Who do you think could have done all that, Dad?"

Mr. Gordon didn't answer. He just stood, gazing at the fire.

Misty could only imagine what her dad was thinking. Did he have any idea what was going on with the *Royal Ashcrumb*?

The phone rang. Misty answered it.

"Hello! Oh my! Hello!" the caller cried. It was Mr. Yates, and he sounded as if someone had dumped ice water down his pants. "Is this a young Gordon? I need to speak to your father. Is he home?"

"Yeah, hold on," said Misty, handing the phone to her dad.

"Yes?" said Mr. Gordon.

Mr. Yates's yelps could be heard over the crackle of the fire. "You must come at once!" Misty heard Mr. Yates saying. "Gone. Just gone!"

"I see," said Mr. Gordon grimly. "I'll be there in a moment." He hung up the phone.

"What's wrong, dear?" Mrs. Gordon asked her husband.

"That was Mr. Yates on the phone," he replied. "An old doublet is missing from the Dearly Departed."

"Missing?" said Mrs. Gordon.

"Oh, I'm sure it's nothing to worry about," Mr. Gordon said. "Mr. Yates probably just misplaced it, that's all. Anyway, I'm going to the store to check on things." He grabbed his coat and slipped out the front door.

Misty and Yoshi looked at each other.

"Where are the scrolls?" whispered Yoshi.

"They're in my room," answered Misty. "I put them in Zaster's vanity."

"What if they were reclaimed, too?" said Yoshi.

The girls scurried upstairs to Misty's bedroom. Yoshi tugged on all the drawers of Madame Zaster's vanity, but they wouldn't budge.

"That's weird," said Yoshi. "It's like these drawers are glued shut."

"Really?" said Misty, walking to the vanity. She put her hand on the drawer containing the scrolls and gave it a slight tug. It glided out with no problem.

Misty breathed a sigh of relief. "The scrolls are still here!"

"But how?" said Yoshi, puzzled, looking at the five scrolls inside the drawer. "How could the scrolls still be here when all the other stuff that was on the *Royal Ashcrumb* was reclaimed? And how did you get that drawer to open?"

"I don't know," said Misty. "It just slid open. Maybe you loosened it . . . or maybe since this is Zaster's vanity, her ghost is protecting the scrolls."

Misty took out Captain Yates's sea chart and unfurled it.

"Oh no!" said the girls together as they spied the tiny painting of the *Royal Ashcrumb*. Only now, instead of being moored at England, the ship was nearly a quarter of the way across the Atlantic Ocean.

"It's moving fast!" cried Misty.

"Look," noticed Yoshi. "You can actually *see* the sails billowing as it moves westward."

"That means somebody's steering it," said Misty, matter-of-factly. She put on Madame Zaster's glasses. They grew colder and foggier than ever before. Misty gasped to see dozens of tiny, pale blue specks crawling all over the ship.

"What do you see?" said Yoshi, breathlessly.

"The ghost crew," said Misty, gazing at the ship in dread. "The *Royal Ashcrumb* has become a sort of ghost ship."

"What do you mean . . . *sort* of ghost ship?" said Yoshi.

"The ship is now like Fannie Belcher's coat," surmised Misty. "We can both see the fur coat and ship because they're real, but ghosts are in control of them—ghosts that I can only see with Madame Zaster's glasses."

"So the prophecy is definitely coming true," said Yoshi. "The ghosts of the Black Adders—the Snakes—have reclaimed the ship. They've set sail from the ship's original starting point in England and are headed our way."

Misty nodded. "I just wonder how much time we have before it gets here."

"Well," said Yoshi, "judging by how far it's already traveled since being 'reclaimed,' we only have three or four days—at most—before the Black Adders come ashore!"

Having seen enough, Misty removed Madame Zaster's glasses, and the phantom crew disappeared from her view.

"Misty!" Mrs. Gordon called up the stairs. "I'm taking James to kung fu class. We'll be back in an hour or so!"

"Okay!" Misty shouted as she put the scrolls back in the drawer. She crossed to the window and watched her mother and James drive off. "This is perfect!" she told Yoshi. "I want to use the crystal ball."

The girls crept downstairs, surprised to find that Mr. Gordon's study was already open and obviously waiting for them, with great billows of fog pouring from it.

Misty took a deep breath. "Come on, let's go," she told Yoshi, and they passed together through the mist and into the room, where the crystal ball sat atop the séance table, gleaming like a globe of ice.

The girls shivered as the ghostly voice of Madame Zaster drifted around the table. "*Sit*," the voice whispered.

The girls quickly took a seat next to each other.

"*Missssty*," said the voice, "*bring your hands to the crystal ball and ask it what you wish to know*."

Misty glanced at Yoshi cluelessly and said under her breath, "Good grief, what do I ask it first? There are so many things . . ."

A foggy finger gave Misty a soft poke in the arm. "*Hurry and ask the ball . . . before it grows dim*," urged the voice.

Misty brought her hands to the glowing orb and simply declared, "Show me where the Golden Three are buried."

Suddenly, the table began to rock angrily, sending the crystal ball rolling wildly across its top toward the edge. Misty stopped the ball just in time.

"*It's not that easy, Misty Gordon!*" said the voice sternly as Misty clutched the ball in fright. "*As I told you before . . . All will be revealed once you have learned the nature of the Golden Three!*"

"Nature?" said Misty, shooting Yoshi a desperate, help-me-out-here look.

"You have to find out the *character* of the Golden Three!" Yoshi explained loudly over the rocking table. "What they're capable of with their powers over the earth, sky, and sea! Perhaps it's something you have to see for yourself to understand!"

And just like that, the table grew still.

"*Well said,*" the voice commended Yoshi. Then it swirled around Misty. "*Try again, Misty.*"

Quivering, Misty put the crystal ball back in place and said, "First, I would like to *see* what happened the day the *Royal Ashcrumb* was taken over by the Black Adders."

Instantly, the crystal ball grew to twice its normal size and began filling with what looked like a sparkling blue liquid. Halfway up the ball, the water stopped rising. Clouds appeared and swirled above the liquid, stirring the water around and around, until tiny waves were rippling in the crystal ball.

"It looks like the ocean," said Misty, amazed.

Just then, Mr. Gordon's radio clicked on, filling the room with the sound of whistling wind. Misty and Yoshi watched in astonishment as a ship appeared upon the ocean.

"It's the *Royal Ashcrumb*," whispered Yoshi.

Over the radio, the ship could be heard splashing through the waves. It was like watching a ship-in-a-bottle, though this particular ship happened to be sailing with a crew aboard!

A tall, noble-looking gentleman stood at the helm. He was wearing a very familiar-looking black doublet. To his side stood a man checking a map with some instruments.

"Straight ahead, Captain Yates," the man with the map said in an English accent. "Ashcrumb is straight ahead, Sir."

"Very good, Officer Monger," said the captain, pleased at this news. "It will be a great relief to successfully deliver King Charles's treasures. Transporting them has not come without considerable risk."

Officer Monger nodded seriously.

Another man approached the captain. "Captain Yates," he said. "We've just spotted a ship headed toward us, Sir. It's gaining fast."

"Ship?" said the captain. "Are you certain, Officer Belcher?"

"Yes, Sir," replied the officer as a pitch-black ship moved into view behind them.

"Oh no," said the captain grimly, checking his spyglass. "The Black Adders have found us." The captain spun around and ordered his crew. "Load guns!"

The crew of sixty was sent into action, with men tearing down below to man the cannons, while the rest scattered about the deck, preparing for the worst, as the Black Adders' devilish ship sped alongside the *Royal Ashcrumb*, so close now that its sails could be heard snapping furiously in the wind, its ragged snake-and-skull flag bearing down upon the royal vessel.

"Fire!" shouted Captain Yates.

Thunderous blasts shot from the cannons, and smoke filled the crystal ball. Though nothing could be seen through the haze, plenty could be heard—pistol shots, voices crying out in agony, and more cannon fire.

"Look," said Yoshi after a while. "The smoke is clearing."

And when it cleared, Misty screamed. For now standing at the helm of the *Royal Ashcrumb* was the grisly man whose ghost she'd seen in the Dearly Departed. He held in his hand a knife, its blade covered in blood. At his feet lay Captain Yates, his throat slit. The sinister killer was obviously the leader of the Black Adders, for behind him stood his gang, pistols jammed into their belts. They were panting from the fight and smiling victoriously. Two men staggered up, carrying a chest.

"Here it is," they said, dropping the chest at the leader's feet. "It was down below."

The leader drew his pistol, fired at the lock on the chest, and kicked it open. His eyes flickered as he dropped to his knees.

"The Golden Three!" he cried, gloating over the gleaming statues and their accompanying scrolls. "'Tis what the Snakes have been dreaming of! With these statues, the Snakes will have complete rule o'er everything! But," he said, closing the lid upon the treasure, "we'll have time for the Golden Three later. We've got to get to Ashcrumb."

He snatched up Captain Yates's maps and began looking them over. "If King Charles was transporting this priceless loot, there's no telling what kind of treasure we might find ashore," he said greedily. Then he turned to his men and grinned wickedly. "And the only way we'll be allowed to *come* ashore is if the colonists think we're English. So remove their attire," he said, gesturing to the lifeless bodies strewn about the deck, "and put it on yourselves. Then, throw the bodies overboard."

The leader began removing the doublet from Captain Yates.

Suddenly, the study became icy cold, as if someone had opened all the windows. In an instant, the fog vanished, the crystal ball dimmed, and the radio went dead.

"Wait," Misty cried. "I'm not done yet!"

"Misty!" Mrs. Gordon called. "We're home. Where are you, dear?"

The girls dashed out of the study and into the kitchen.

"You're back already?" said Misty.

"Yes," said Mrs. Gordon. "James's kung fu class had been canceled. Tell them why, James," she added with a smile.

"Because it's snowing!" he cheered, doing a kick.

"It's snowing?" the girls cried together.

They quickly pulled on their coats and hats and ran outside into the quiet snowfall, twirling in the white fluff that was falling from the evening sky.

Misty smiled. There was nothing like snow to take your mind off your worries. "Let it snow, let it snow, let it snow!" she sang.

12

The Field Trip

And snow it did! It snowed all night long, turning Ashcrumb into a winter wonderland. Despite the glistening, cheerful landscape that greeted her the next morning, Misty's mind couldn't have been any gloomier as she set out with Yoshi and James for their walk to school. She was just obsessing darkly on the ghost ship, its wicked crew, and Fannie Belcher's ghastly threat when someone called out from a passing vehicle.

"Hey, want a ride?"

It was Hector Figg, his head sticking out from his father's slick silver van.

"Sure!" everyone replied, jumping inside. The interior of the van was just like the cockpit of an airplane, with lots of panels and blinking lights.

"So, when is the new lighthouse going to be ready, Dr. Figg?" asked Yoshi.

"Oh, you'll find out all about the lighthouse today," he replied, glancing at the dashboard and flipping some switches. "I'll be filling you in on everything."

"How's that?" said Misty, finally jogging her mind from its worries.

"Your class is taking a field trip to the lighthouse this morning," Dr. Figg said. "I'm giving you and your classmates a personal, guided tour!"

Misty and Yoshi grinned. Field trips were the best.

"Here we are," said Dr. Figg, pulling in front of the castle.

"We'll see you later, Dr. Figg," said Misty as they all poured out of the van.

"Affirmative," he replied, adjusting his headset.

The van's door shut with a whir and off the van went, blinking and buzzing.

"OKAY, SINGLE FILE! LET'S HURRY! WE'VE GOT A SCHEDULE TO KEEP," Coach Knuckles directed through his megaphone as Misty's class climbed aboard a school bus for the field trip. "NO EATING OR DRINKING. HEY, I SEE THOSE POTATO CHIPS. DROP THEM RIGHT NOW, BUSTER!"

"Oh great," Misty moaned once aboard. "All the good seats are taken."

Yoshi and Misty took the last available—and broken—back-row seat.

"Did you bring a puke bag?" whispered Yoshi.

Misty nodded, pulling a paper sack from her bag. Misty happened to be quite a puker, and nothing made her woozier than rides on school buses. That's why she always walked to school.

"You may as well get that bag ready," advised Yoshi as the bus's engine cranked on. "Because it looks like Mr. Barrel is going to be doing the driving. With his nerves, there's no telling what we're in for."

As it turned out, they were in for something very, very bad. Vice Principal Barrel was the nuttiest driver in the world. To make matters worse, Coach Knuckles was the worst *backseat* driver in the universe. He sat directly behind Mr. Barrel the entire ride, shouting at him through the megaphone.

"WATCH OUT!" he'd yell, giving Mr. Barrel's seat a thump. "There's a SQUIRREL!"

"Jeez," Mr. Barrel would wince, swerving onto the sidewalk before swinging back onto the road.

"Is Misty Gordon gagging yet?" Alexis Lenox laughed from the front row.

Coach Knuckles spun around and blared at Misty, who was turning green. "TOUGH IT OUT, GORDON! PUT YOUR HEAD BETWEEN YOUR LEGS AND TAKE A DEEP BREATH!"

"Oh no," Misty groaned, throwing her head between her knees, catching a glimpse of a moldy french fry rolling around on the bus floor. "This is the *worst*."

"LET'S GET A MOVE ON!" Coach Knuckles thundered. "PUNCH IT, BARREL!"

Mr. Barrel mashed the accelerator, sending everyone shooting forward in their seats.

"Hey, there's Margie Medford!" someone cried as the bus passed the asylum, where Medford was waiting like the Abominable Snowman. A seasoned crossing guard, her ears were finely tuned to the sound of approaching school buses. She dashed to the gate and fired off a round of snowballs through the iron bars of the asylum's fence. "You'll be seeing me again!" she swore as snowballs smacked against the bus windows. "I'll be baaaaaack!"

The startled students shrank into their seats, and there they stayed until reaching the lighthouse.

"Gather around," Mr. Barrel said after the students filed from the bus. He did a head count. "Where's Misty Gordon?"

Misty slowly emerged from the bus, her barf bag in her hand. She hadn't needed to use it after all, but she'd come awfully close, especially over that last bridge.

"Come on, time's a wasting," said Mr. Barrel. "Lots to see and learn on this field trip."

Dr. Figg appeared in a lab coat alongside the group in the parking lot. He gestured proudly toward the tall, gleaming white structure that stretched into the clouds. "Kids, just look at this lighthouse!" he declared. "She's the first of her kind. A supreme, high-tech scientific piece of equipment. And she happens to have a heck of a lightbulb, too. But I'm getting ahead of myself. Everyone, follow me to the elevator."

The students stepped through the doors and onto a platform. "Hang on," Dr. Figg told everyone as he pushed a button. Up shot the platform, whisking the students to the building's upper story so quickly that they were airborne for a second. Misty felt her stomach rise and churn.

"Easy does it, partner," Coach Knuckles told Misty.

The doors whooshed open, and the students trooped into

a round room, where a dozen men in technician's coats were whisking back and forth with clipboards in hand. In the center of the room was a huge control panel aglow with pale green grids and thousands of buttons.

"This is the brain center of the lighthouse," said Dr. Figg. "This is where we monitor any movement at sea for hundreds of miles. Talk about a view, ay?"

Everyone looked out the window that curved around the entire room. It really was a sight to see. They were up so high that the dark waves of the Atlantic seemed to stretch to infinity. The old lighthouse, which stood on the opposite side of the bay, looked like a toy.

"See that boat out there?" said Dr. Figg, pointing out the window toward a tiny speck on the horizon. "Well, here it is on this grid." He then pointed to a control panel where a white point blinked against an incandescent green screen.

"That blinking dot represents that boat on the horizon. According to this grid, the boat is approximately six miles away. But, thanks to SALLIE, we're able to get even more specific than that."

"Who's SALLIE?" asked Mr. Barrel.

"SALLIE is our supercomputer," said Dr. Figg. "It stands for Spectrum Activated Lighthouse with Laser Investigative Electromagnetics. Allow me to demonstrate."

Dr. Figg rattled off an order into his headset. "SALLIE, give me a sector scan on northeast quadrant, including full-spectrum onboard data."

SALLIE's cool, electronic voice sounded in the room: "Boat is a yacht. Forty feet in length, heading due north at fifteen knots. Passengers include four male humans, three female humans, and a small dog."

"What *kind* of dog?" said Dr. Figg, dramatically.

"Teacup poodle," answered SALLIE.

Gasps filled the room. Dr. Figg nodded triumphantly.

"SALLIE can detect any object for hundreds of miles. If anything moves out *there*," he said, pointing at the ocean, "it shows up *here*," he said, then pointing at the grid.

"Try something else!" blurted Mike Finn. "Like that seagull that's flying past the window."

"Sure," said Dr. Figg enthusiastically, eager to show off the supercomputer. "SALLIE, give me an aerial scan of approaching seagull."

Again, the electronic voice sounded: "Male seagull, wingspan twenty-eight inches, flying in a downward spiral of ten feet per second. Projected time to crash-landing on beach . . . two-point-five seconds."

Everyone watched as the clumsy bird—as predicted—tumbled headfirst into a snow-covered sand dune below.

Cheers went up. Dr. Figg smiled, and his team of technicians clapped.

"Once the lighthouse is fully operational," continued Dr. Figg, "things will really get interesting. If anything is detected out there in the dark of night or thick fog, the lighthouse will automatically hone in on the moving object with its zillion-watt superbeam. All in all, this system gives us plenty of time to discover what is headed our way and to keep ships from crashing ashore. Don't touch that button, kid," Dr. Figg added, brushing a sticky hand from the control panel.

"When do we get to see SALLIE's superbeam?" asked Yoshi.

"I was just getting to that," said Dr. Figg. "There is going to be a lighting ceremony this Friday night. And at this very moment, I am going to choose a lucky person who will have the honor of throwing the switch! Who of you might be interested?"

Hands shot into the air and began waving wildly. Alexis Lenox bullied her way through the crowd, knocking down Mike Finn, elbowing Chris Connors, and even pinching Jasmine O'Malley as she cut a clear path to Dr. Figg. She threw her arms in the air and began jumping, her red ponytail slapping Misty's face.

"Pick me!" Alexis shrieked.

"And the lucky person is . . . ," Dr. Figg said thoughtfully, scanning the heads.

"Oooooh, I'm right here!" Alexis called, tugging Dr. Figg's lab coat.

"And the lucky person is," Dr. Figg repeated, "Misty Gordon!"

The crowd slumped and sighed all together. Alexis glared at Misty. In return, Misty gave her a big smile.

⌒

The walk home from school was dark and cold. Misty and Yoshi scooted down the sidewalk, their heads buried in their coats, while James and Hector trotted in front of the girls, stopping at every lawn to scoop up a handful of snow to throw at each other.

As they passed the front of the Monger mansion, James packed a big snowball in his gloves and cried, "Hey, watch me peg Hazel Monger's door with this thing!"

"James, you better not," said Misty, looking warily over the mansion's iron fence.

"Why?" said James. "Hazel's not outside. She'll never know, man."

"Throw it, James!" said Hector. "See if you can hit the door knocker."

"Be quiet," said James. "I gotta concentrate."

Leaning against the fence, James drew his arm back and then hurled the snowball at the black door.

"You missed!" laughed Hector.

"Come on, let's go," said Misty, pulling on James's coat. "It's freezing out here."

"Let me try once more," said James, scooping up a slushy ball of ice from the sidewalk and packing it tight. "Here it goes. Watch this!"

With a running start, he drew back the snowball and flung it over the fence. It landed on the door knocker with a loud *THUD*.

"Score!" shouted James victoriously.

In an instant, the door flew open and Hazel Monger tore out of the mansion.

"BRATS!" she shrieked. Hazel reached into her bag of rocks and flung a handful at them.

They ducked, and the rocks scattered across the sidewalk.

"Yaaaahhh!" Hazel screamed, clattering down the steps and coming through the snow toward them, her face reddening with rage. She stuck her hand in the bag, pulled out another fistful of rocks, and launched them at the children.

"Missed again!" Hector shouted.

Ranting, Hazel thrust her hand into the bag again. Seconds passed as she stood knee-deep in snow, her black shawl fluttering in the wind as she felt impatiently around in the bag for some more rocks.

"Out of ammo, aren't ya?" James yelled tauntingly.

Hazel glared at the children, her snaky eyes twitching.

And what happened next was completely unexpected.

For Hazel Monger, realizing that she had no more rocks to throw, went into an inner temper tantrum. Filled with anger, she turned the color of a stewed tomato and began vibrating, as if she were a pot simmering atop a stove. She gave a short jump, and then, before everyone's astonished eyes, little wisps of smoke began pouring from her bright red ears.

"I think Hazel's about to blow," declared Yoshi.

And she did. Literally. Having met her boiling point, Hazel Monger exploded in a quick, bright burst of yellow flames, as if a ray gun from outer space had blasted her. Everyone covered their eyes. When they looked back, Hazel was nothing more than ashes atop a puddle of melted snow.

To say the least, the shocking spectacle left Misty and James without an appetite for dinner that evening. But their parents, who hadn't witnessed the human volcano, actually brought their meals into the living room and ate from TV trays while they waited for the local news to come on.

"Shh, here it is," said Mr. Gordon, his eyes glued to the television.

"Day turned tragic," said the reporter, "when local woman Hazel Monger perished in a fire that investigators are calling mysterious. That's right, mysterious! Listen up, folks!"

Mr. and Mrs. Gordon leaned forward, perched on the edge of their seats.

"It's science fiction come to life," exclaimed the reporter. "After a thorough investigation, experts determined that Hazel Monger spontaneously exploded. This rare phenomenon, when the human body actually catches itself ablaze, was the source of the fire and resulting cause of Monger's death. As with many victims of spontaneous human combustion, Hazel Monger was instantly and completely incinerated." The reporter shivered and then smiled plastically. "Reporting for ATVE, I'm Tom Blotswell!"

Mrs. Gordon turned off the TV.

"Well," said Mr. Gordon, "the old witch is finally dead."

"So . . . ," wondered James, "does that mean you're gonna get some of her stuff in her mansion tomorrow?"

"Unfortunately, no," said Mr. Gordon. "I learned this afternoon that Hazel Monger was very clear about the handling of her estate upon her death. In her will, she explicitly stated that . . . that . . ."—Mr. Gordon started to chuckle—". . . that her 'mansion and its contents be left alone after her death until she can figure out what to do with them.'"

"You *have* to be kidding," howled Mrs. Gordon. "Sounds like Hazel Monger thought she would live forever . . . or *at least come back from the dead.*"

"How crazy!" laughed James.

Misty swallowed and sank into the couch. It didn't sound so crazy to *her*.

Even though the Gordons' company truck did not visit the Monger mansion the next day, it still had been put to good use, as Misty, Yoshi, and James discovered after their walk home from school. For as they trudged up the driveway, they glimpsed the tip of a Christmas tree hanging out the back of the ice-cream truck.

"All right!" James cheered. "Dad got the Christmas tree!"

"Are you kidding?" laughed Yoshi, shocked. "It's only the second week of November! It's way too early for Christmas trees!"

"You don't understand," Misty explained to Yoshi. "When you're in the retail business like my family is, the moment Halloween's over, it's all about the holidays."

"She's right," added James. "Our parents always decorate the Dearly Departed and our house at the same time."

They found Mrs. Gordon in the garage, surrounded by boxes of Christmas decorations.

"Oh good!" she said, peering over a plastic elf. "You kids are home. We're going to be decorating this evening. Lots to do."

"Catch!" Mr. Gordon called down from the attic. He dropped a wad of string lights down to Misty and Yoshi. "See if you girls can get those things untangled."

While the girls worked on getting the knots out of the lights, Misty noticed a metal detector leaning in the corner of the garage next to the Vespa.

"Whose metal detector?" asked Misty.

"Oh," coughed Mr. Gordon. "That's mine. I found it in the attic while I was digging around. I thought I might see if the thing still works."

"Speaking of working," said Misty, having untangled a string of colored lights and plugging it in. "These still work. Check it out."

"Wonderful," said Mrs. Gordon, clapping her hands. "Now, let's get to decorating."

A few hours later, the tree had been moved into the house, strung with lights, and completely decorated. Outside, hundreds of strands of lights twinkled in the bushes, and a large wooden Santa and elves stood in the front yard next to a six-foot-tall Christmas card that read:

Happy Holidays!
From your local D.E.A.D.

Mrs. Gordon, Misty, Yoshi, and James stood outside, admiring their handiwork.

"It's beautiful," gushed Mrs. Gordon. "Simply beautiful! Misty, go inside and get your father. Tell him to come look at this masterpiece!"

"Dad isn't inside," said James.

"Then where is he?" asked Mrs. Gordon.

"I saw him sneak off down the street with that metal detector," said James.

"Girls, go see if you can find him," said Mrs. Gordon. "He can't be that far."

"Oh, all right," sighed Misty.

The girls walked out of the lighted yard into the darkness of the neighborhood. They looked one way down the road and then the other, but Mr. Gordon was nowhere to be seen.

"Where could he have gone?" asked Yoshi. "And what in the world would he be doing out in the cold night with a metal detector?"

"I have no idea," grumbled Misty. "Let's just walk a little further, and then we'll turn around."

They ambled on. "Wait, I hear something," said Yoshi.

The girls stopped in their tracks and listened to a *BEEP! WHIRRR! WHOOP!*

The noises were coming from up ahead. Misty and Yoshi slinked through two front yards, then stopped. They were right on top of the beeps. And they were also right in front of the late Hazel Monger's dark and empty mansion. Strangely, the noises were coming from the deserted home's backyard. What was going on back there?

Misty opened the iron gate just a bit and they squeezed through, careful not to let it creak. Then they rushed to the backyard and peeked over a wall of bushes.

Misty gasped.

For there was her father, moving the metal detector over the frozen earth of dead Hazel Monger's yard.

13

All Is Revealed

Mrs. Gordon, Misty, and James had all eaten dinner that evening, and Mr. Gordon had not returned. And hours later, after Mrs. Gordon and James had gone to bed, there were still no signs of Mr. Gordon.

In the dark living room, Misty lay awake on the couch, waiting for her father. She knew that if there was a time to talk to her dad about the Golden Three, this was it. Finally, when the grandfather clock in the hall chimed at midnight, the front door creaked open.

"Oh, goodness!" Mr. Gordon said, startled to see Misty. "What are you doing up at this hour?"

Misty stared at him. "Dad, I know where you've been tonight," she said in a hushed voice. "And what's more . . . I know what you've been looking for."

Mr. Gordon sat down in his chair. He took a deep breath. "So, tell me then. What am I looking for?"

"The Golden Three," Misty replied.

Mr. Gordon's eyes opened wide. "How did you know that?"

"It's a long story," said Misty.

"I've got all night," he said, leaning back in the chair. "So tell me your story."

And Misty told him about Madame Zaster's ghost; Fannie Belcher's diary and coat; the ghosts in the Dearly Departed; discovering that Fannie Belcher, Hazel Monger, and Mr. Yates were the last three Descendants of the Black Adders; the crystal ball; the enchanted radio in his study; the phone call from Fannie Belcher; and the prophecy. She told him everything.

Mr. Gordon listened, sinking more and more into the mushy chair, dropping into shadow until all that could be seen of him was a glimmering reflection of firelight in his eyeglasses.

It was two o'clock in the morning when Misty finished her story.

"So even though you've been searching for the Golden Three all these years, it's more important—and urgent—than ever to find them," said Misty. "The ghosts of the Black Adders are returning, and if they or any of their descendants find the

Golden Three, then incredibly bad stuff is going to happen. For starters, Fannie Belcher is going to get me! And then the Black Adders will destroy the town!"

Mr. Gordon held up his hand. "Okay, okay," he said. "I've heard plenty."

Misty grew hush.

There was a quiet pause, in which Mr. Gordon rubbed his eyes behind his glasses and scratched his chin. "Misty," he finally said, "this is a lot to swallow. I knew that the Golden Three were buried somewhere in town. And yes, I wanted to find them. I was very poor, so you can imagine just how much I wanted to get my hands on that treasure."

"But you don't believe the prophecy?" Misty said, exasperated.

"Listen, Misty," said Mr. Gordon. "When I was a boy and spied on the séance at Madame Zaster's cottage, I did overhear the prophecy. I admit that when I first heard it, it sounded frightening, but as I've grown older, I realize that it was hocus-pocus nonsense. And this other stuff you're talking about . . . it's just so farfetched! I mean, *pirates*?" At this, he started to chuckle but quickly stopped once he saw the solemn look on Misty's face.

"So you don't believe me?" said Misty.

"I'm still trying to grasp the notion that old Mr. Yates is a descendant of a pirate," he snickered. "It's one of the funniest things I've ever heard. And you say," he added, "that Mr. Yates even had maps? That's too much." He gave a deep, belly-shaking laugh.

"Yes," said Misty, firmly. "Mr. Yates did have maps, and I'll prove it." She stood up. "The maps are in my room. I'll show you."

She led her father to her room, where she crouched next to Madame Zaster's vanity and tried to open the drawer containing the scrolls.

It wouldn't open.

"Come on, open," she said, pulling on the handle. But it wouldn't budge.

She shot an embarrassed look at her father, who stood, arms folded and eyebrows raised.

"I'm not making this all up," insisted Misty. "I'm sure it does sound—"

"Crazy? Ridiculous?" he said, no longer laughing. "It sure does."

"You have to believe me," said Misty, tears of frustration welling up in her eyes. "If I can just get to the crystal ball one more time, I can figure this all out and find the Golden Three."

"Right, right," snorted Mr. Gordon, rolling his eyes. "The crystal ball." He shook his head. "You know, I can't say I'm too happy with you going into my study, now that I think of it."

"Sorry about that," winced Misty. "But if you don't believe in the powers of the crystal ball, then why did you keep it in your study, along with the séance table? Why didn't you take it to the Dearly Departed?"

"Because there wasn't any *room* for it at the Dearly Departed," replied Mr. Gordon. "It's as simple as that."

He patted Misty on the head. "It's time to go to bed."

Misty knew the tone in her father's voice. It was a tone he used when he told her what she wanted to hear but wasn't really listening to what she had to say.

Misty curled up on her bed, accepting the fact that her dad thought she was off her rocker. Obviously, he hadn't bought a thing she'd said. She yawned, her eyelids suddenly becoming very, very heavy.

"Sweet dreams," he said, walking out of her room.

But that night, Misty would have anything but sweet dreams.

She dreamed she was flying over the ocean, soaring over the dark waves of the Atlantic. She could feel the cold wind in her hair as she dipped and glided as if she were a bird. She could see something below riding the choppy surface of the water. It was a ship. Misty flew in for a closer look and read the name across its stern: *Royal Ashcrumb.* The ship's sails fluttered as the vessel crashed through the waves. Misty floated past the men on deck. There stood the leader of the Black Adders at the helm, wearing the doublet. In his bloody hands he held the Golden Three. Closer still Misty flew to him, until she could see every long, greasy, black hair on his dirty head, the flicker of evil in his eyes, and the sinister smile on his crooked mouth, which slowly opened and hissed, "'Tis what the Snakes have been dreamin' of."

Misty awoke with a scream. She sat up, her heart racing.

"It was just a nightmare," she said, pulling her quilt over her head.

Suddenly, a voice said, "What do you mean *nightmare*? It's a miracle!"

Misty lowered the quilt to see James standing at the foot of her bed, jumping up and down.

"*Miracle?*" said Misty.

"Yeah, it's a miracle," he cheered, pointing out the window. "School's been canceled because of all the snow!"

Misty got up and looked. Sure enough, it was a complete whiteout.

"Hector and I are going ice-skating at Lenox Lake," James said. "Dr. Figg is taking us. Mom and Dad are going, too, so if you wanna come, you better hurry up, because we're leaving in fifteen minutes."

Misty realized this would be a perfect time to visit the crystal ball. "I think I'll stay here," she said.

"Suit yourself," said James, leaving the room.

Misty dressed and went to the kitchen, where everyone was finishing up breakfast.

"My goodness, Misty!" said her mother. "You look tired."

"I didn't get much sleep last night," yawned Misty.

"Why not?" asked her mother, handing her a plate.

Before Misty could reply, Mr. Gordon cleared his throat. "It must have been the wind howling," he said, winking at Misty. "The wind kept you up, didn't it?"

"Oh, yeah!" said Misty. "It was the wind."

"I see," said her mother. "Well, are you sure you don't want to come along with us to Lenox Lake for some ice-skating?"

"I'm positive," said Misty. "I'm just going to hang out here. I'll call Yoshi to come over."

"Dr. Figg and Hector are here," James announced, peeking out the window.

James opened the door, and Dr. Figg and Hector stomped inside, swirls of snow sweeping in with them.

"So you're taking off work today, Dr. Figg?" asked Misty.

"Yes," he replied, smiling at Misty. "By the way, are you getting excited about being the designated switch-flipper at the lighting ceremony?"

"Designated switch-flipper?" repeated Mr. Gordon, curiously.

"That's right," said Dr. Figg. "Misty here will have the honor of flipping the switch on the new lighthouse tomorrow evening. Didn't she tell you?"

Misty's parents shook their heads.

"Misty is so humble," offered Mr. Gordon. "She hasn't even mentioned it around here."

"She's shy," added Mrs. Gordon, brushing Misty's bangs from her glasses. "She's at that shy stage."

"Mom," Misty moaned. "*Please*. Besides, the lighting ceremony might also be canceled because of the snow. Right, Dr. Figg?"

"Not a chance of that," he said. "It might have snowed last night, but it's going to be warming up quickly. The forecast for tomorrow calls for clear skies. Yes," he said happily, "the weather conditions are going to be perfect for the ceremony. I think it's going to be quite an evening."

"We can't wait," said Mrs. Gordon. "Well, let's get a move on before all the ice melts away."

"We'll see you later, Misty," said Mr. Gordon as they all filed out the door.

After Dr. Figg's van cruised away, Misty called Yoshi on the phone.

"Get over here," she told Yoshi. "Everybody's gone, so we can use the crystal ball one last time."

Five minutes later, Misty and Yoshi found themselves entering the foggy doorway of Mr. Gordon's study and taking their seats next to each other at the séance table, where the crystal ball was glowing brighter than ever.

Misty was just reaching for the crystal ball when the fog began to pour itself into a chair opposite them.

The girls watched, dumbstruck, as the smoky vapors grew thicker and thicker until forming the shape of a person.

"Is that you, Madame Zaster?" said Yoshi, gaping at the hazy figure.

The ghost nodded.

Misty leaned forward, puzzled. "How can Yoshi and I *both* see you?"

"*The Unseen is illuminated in the glow of the crystal,*" explained Madame Zaster, looking at the girls and then at the gleaming ball. "*Misty, bring your hands to the crystal,*" she said. "*Tell it what else you would like to know.*"

Misty brought her hands to the ball and said, "I want to see what happened when the Black Adders came ashore with the Golden Three."

The orb trembled atop the table and started to grow—larger than ever—while filling with deep blue liquid. Again, the sound of the wind came over the radio as the ocean within the orb began to ripple. In a flicker, the *Royal Ashcrumb* appeared atop the waves. Upon her deck was the ship's new and deadly crew: the Black Adders.

Now all wearing their victims' attire, the disguised pirate crew was busy atop the deck, minding the sails, while their leader (wearing the captain's garb) and his two henchmen (outfitted in the officers' attire) discussed their plans.

"We're nearing Ashcrumb Bay," the leader said, peering through a spyglass. "We'll be making land at dusk."

Over the wind came the gong of a bell.

"What's that?" asked one of his henchmen.

"We've been spotted," said the leader. "Our arrival has been signaled. The colonists will be waiting for us."

"Aye, Captain," chuckled the phony officer.

"That's Captain *Yates*," reminded the leader. "You must remember to call me Captain Yates," he growled. He looked at the sham officers. "And your names are—"

"Officer Benton Belcher," replied one.

"Officer William Monger," answered the other.

"And don't forget it," warned the captain brutishly, shoving his long hair beneath his hat. "For our plan to work, the colonists must believe we are the crew of the *Royal Ashcrumb*." He checked the long line of buttons on his doublet and then drew his bloodstained ruff over his neck, covering his Black Adders tattoo.

The captain looked down and grinned. At his feet lay the chest containing the Golden Three and their scrolls. He kicked open the lid and lifted out one of the statues, while Monger unfurled and read the scrolls.

"So, those things have magic powers, ay?" Belcher croaked to the captain.

The sham captain nodded gloatingly.

"What does that one do?" asked Belcher, pointing to the statue the captain was holding.

"This is Zeus," said the captain gruffly. "He controls the sky."

"And this one?" asked Belcher, pulling out another statue.

"That's Poseidon," answered the captain. "God of the sea."

Belcher extracted the last statue. "And what about this one?" he asked. "He's a mean-lookin' devil."

"That's Hades," said the captain, obviously impressed with this particular statue. "He rules the underworld. The dead. With him, the dead can be awakened."

"Let's see if they work!" Monger barked, snatching the statue of Poseidon from Belcher's grasp. Monger hoisted the statue in the air and commanded, "Poseidon, pass your power through me!"

Instantly, the skies grew dark. Black clouds began to boil above the ship, and up came a fierce, howling wind, pitching the ship on her side.

"GIVE ME THOSE!" shouted the captain, throwing the statues back into the chest. Then he grabbed the scrolls from

Monger and tucked them inside his doublet with the maps just as rain began lashing the sails.

The captain called out orders to his crew, trying to steady the ship, but it was to no avail. Within seconds, the hellish storm was bearing down upon the vessel. With a searing blast, a streak of lightning spidered from the sky and struck the mast. Terrible sounds followed: the crackle of splintering wood, the roar of fire, the hissing of water as parts of the blazing ship tumbled into the waves.

Misty stared into the crystal ball and commanded, "Let me watch the rest from ashore."

The crystal ball flickered, and the view changed. As if she were standing on the shore herself, Misty was now watching the ship burning in the bay.

The sham captain and his two officers staggered ashore, their silhouettes outlined in firelight. Holding tight to the chest, the captain watched as the fire and waves continued their wrath upon the ship and the rest of his crew.

Just then, a streak of lightning struck the Bell Tower, sending a red-hot charge to its huge bell. For a moment, the bell blazed bloodred. In its crimson glow, the tower's watchman could be seen way down the beach, running from the tower's base toward the captain and his officers.

Still clutching the chest, the captain tore into some trees

beyond the beach. Quickly, he took out the statues. "Keep an eye on that watchman," he ordered as he sunk the statues deep in the slushy dirt among the tree roots.

"Why don't we just kill the watchman?" asked Belcher.

"With *what*?" snarled the captain, tossing the chest behind the trees. "Our pistols are spent . . . and our swords are at the bottom of the bay! Besides, he's sounded the bell. Colonists will be coming any moment, and they might be armed.

"Remember our plan," he croaked. "After we find more loot in King Charles's castle, then we'll leave Ashcrumb. We'll take one of the colony's boats and haul away."

"And what about the Golden Three?" asked Monger.

"We'll dig 'em up on our way out of here," answered the captain.

"Quiet!" said Monger as the watchman approached the trees. "Looks like the bloke's found us."

"Hello? Anybody there?" called the watchman urgently as he parted the leaves. "Are you there? Are you all right?"

The watchman's eyes opened wide as the captain emerged from the trees, his devilish face glowing red with firelight, his long hair twisting in the wind. The watchman backed up and then squinted suspiciously at the sinister-looking man.

"Halt!" shouted the watchman, drawing his pistol. "Identify yourself!"

"Captain Yates," the impostor declared, tugging on his doublet importantly as a group of colonists appeared and gathered around. "I am Captain Nicholas Yates!" he repeated loudly, his chin in the air. "Captain of His Majesty's Ship, the *Royal Ashcrumb*, which has succumbed to the storm!" He faked a distraught expression, tossing his hands in the air toward the sinking ship. "Most of my crew has been lost! Lost!" He shook his head miserably. "But a few of my officers have survived," he added as the two counterfeit officers crept forward. "They are Officer Belcher and Officer Monger."

For a moment, the watchman stood, his pistol still raised, as he and the colonists looked the captain and officers up and down. Still not entirely convinced of their claim, the watchman looked at the captain and asked, "What proof have you?"

With oily relish, the captain pulled the sea chart from his doublet, unfurled it, and turned it to the light of the fire. "Behold, proof!" he declared, holding it up for all to see. "This is the map by which I guided the *Royal Ashcrumb* across the Atlantic to the Royal Colony of Ashcrumb by order of the High and Mighty King of England!"

The watchman and colonists leaned over and had a look at the map. Then, giving a final glance at the captain's and his officers' attire, the watchman lowered his pistol.

Another violent streak of lightning bolted from the sky and

struck the trees behind them. The tree under which the statues had been buried instantly burst into flames. The captain and officers watched as the entire shoreline caught ablaze, the trees exploding in flames.

"The storm is getting worse!" yelled a colonist. "We must head inland! All's lost here!"

The captain and officers wouldn't budge. They just stood, staring at the spot where they'd buried the Golden Three.

"Come on!" yelled the watchman, pulling at the captain. "You'll die out here!"

Cursing beneath their breath, the captain and officers reluctantly followed the colonists. Reaching the top of a dune, the captain turned to glimpse—in utter dismay—an enormous wave crashing upon the shore, wiping out everything in its path.

"Looks like we'll be in Ashcrumb for a time," the captain muttered to his officers as another wave tore away more of the shore. "There's no telling where the statues will end up after this storm." He squinted his dark eyes and pledged. "But no matter how long it takes to find them, we'll search for the Golden Three."

A cold wind whirled through the study. The crystal ball and radio went dead.

"*You have* seen *much*," said Madame Zaster, her foggy image growing faint. "*You have learned the nature of the Golden Three.*"

"Wait!" Misty cried. "Don't go! I still don't know where the Golden Three ended up! You know I've got to find them before the Snakes come ashore!"

Madame Zaster's ghost could now barely be seen.

Yoshi piped up. "If the Snakes find them before Misty does, she's doomed!"

"Forget me!" Misty said to Yoshi. "What about our entire *town*?"

The glow of Madame Zaster's ghost grew stronger, and for the first time, the apparition smiled.

"*Well done, Misty Gordon,*" the ghost said, pleased. "*You have proven* your *nature to me.*"

"Huh?" said Misty.

"*You've thought of others instead of yourself or treasure,*" the ghost explained. Then the apparition touched Misty's hand and said, "*The Golden Three were moved from Ashcrumb sand, and now they lie in the palm of your hand.*"

"What do you mean, *moved*?" said Misty. Then her eyes flew open. "So you *did* know where the Golden Three were! You found them, and you moved them from the beach, didn't you?"

"*Yes,*" said Madame Zaster. "*I moved them to a place where the Descendants would never think to look. After all, there was no way that I was going to let such power fall into their despicable hands."*

With that, Madame Zaster turned back into wispy vapors and rose above their heads.

"Remember . . . ," Madame Zaster's voice whispered. *"The Golden Three were moved from Ashcrumb sand . . . and now they lie in the palm of your hand."*

A gust of wind blew through the room, and the fog disappeared.

14

The Lighting Ceremony

For a moment, the stunned girls looked at each other.

"Whoa," said Yoshi, finally. "So Madame Zaster moved the Golden Three. And she even told you where she moved them to!" Yoshi paused, a confused look clouding her face. "I mean . . . she kinda . . . *sorta* told you where she moved them to."

"Right," said Misty, vexed. "All she told us was *another* riddle!"

"I know," said Yoshi. "*The answer lies in the palm of your hand*. What could that mean?"

"I have no idea," said Misty. "But it's obvious that it has to do with these mysterious lines in my hand." Misty glanced at her palm and gasped. "Look, Yoshi!" she said. "There are some new marks!"

Yoshi leaned over and had a look. Sure enough, in the corner of Misty's palm, three tiny, sparkling golden dots had appeared.

"When did you get those?" said Yoshi, intrigued.

"I don't know," said Misty, touching the gleaming points. "Wait a second . . . I bet it was when Madame Zaster's ghost just touched my hand."

"Wow," said Yoshi. "That is amazing."

Misty sighed. "As amazing as it is, we still don't know what it means."

"Well, maybe there's still time to figure it out before the *Royal Ashcrumb* gets here," said Yoshi.

Oh, how Misty hoped her friend was right.

"Well, Dr. Figg was correct about the weather forecast," said Mrs. Gordon cheerfully the next morning as she peered out the kitchen window. She turned and smiled at Misty, who sat alone at the table, picking dismally at her breakfast. "The skies are clear and it's gotten warmer, so it should be a perfect night for the lighting ceremony."

Misty shrugged her shoulders indifferently.

"Aw, come on, now," said Mrs. Gordon. "Don't get nervous about the ceremony."

"I'm not nervous about the ceremony," said Misty glumly. "I just have a lot on my mind."

"Like what?" asked Mrs. Gordon, her hands on her hips.

"Nothing."

"Oh, for gracious sakes," sighed Mrs. Gordon. "Why are you acting so secretive?"

"I am *not* acting secretive," huffed Misty.

"Well, you sure have been acting very mysterious lately," said Mrs. Gordon. "I can't help but notice how you choose to stay in your room instead of going places with your family. And don't roll your eyes."

"Mom, *please*," moaned Misty. "I am *not* acting mysterious."

"Well, you certainly seem to be hiding something," said Mrs. Gordon.

Misty took a deep breath and shook her head.

"Now, about this evening," said Mrs. Gordon. "Hurry home after school. Dr. Figg said that quite a crowd is expected on the beach tonight for the ceremony, so we need to get there a little early. When the time comes for you to go to the lighthouse, Dr. Figg will beep you with this."

Mrs. Gordon handed Misty a little silver pager.

"Just think," said Mrs. Gordon excitedly, "you'll be at the tip-top of the tower. There's no telling what you'll see!"

That afternoon, Misty and Yoshi stood on the beach, huddling around a bonfire with Misty's family.

"I staked out the best spot on the beach," said Mr. Gordon proudly, stoking the fire with a stick of driftwood. "We've got a great view of the new lighthouse."

He gazed up at the lighthouse, which looked like a giant flagpole from the North Pole, the tall white structure having been wrapped festively with a giant red streamer.

Before long the sun was setting. "It will be dark soon," Mr. Gordon told Misty. "Why don't you girls go ask Mr. Yates if he'd like to join us on the beach."

"Yeah, sure," said Misty.

The girls trudged up the dunes to Plunder Street.

"Check it out!" said Yoshi, smiling as they gazed down the street. "It's Christmas Central!"

Nobody knew how to decorate for the holidays like the merchants along Plunder Street. The shop owners had turned the street into a veritable Christmas village. Store windows were aglow with twinkling lights, trees, and decorations. Huge green wreaths hung from lampposts, swags of glimmering tinsel crisscrossed the street, and the sound of bells could be heard jingling in the crisp sea breeze. Despite the festive mood, however, Misty felt gloomier than ever. If only the town knew what was headed its way!

There was a flurry of activity on the street. "I've never seen so many people on Plunder Street in all my life!" said Yoshi.

"They must all be here for the lighting ceremony," said Misty as they funneled their way through the hordes along the sidewalk.

In front of the Sweethouse Candy and Condiments Shop stood Mrs. Sweethouse, this time dressed as Mrs. Santa Claus and handing out cups of hot cocoa.

"Misty Gordon!" she called. "I read in the newspaper that you're going to be throwing the switch at the ceremony. Congratulations!"

Misty blushed as a crowd of people turned and stared. A TV reporter and cameraman bustled up to Misty.

"So you're the lucky girl!" said the reporter. "Mind if we do a quick interview?"

Misty blinked.

"Terrific!" said the reporter, signaling his cameraman to start filming. "I'm standing on Plunder Street with Misty Gordon," he said dramatically in front of the camera. "Tell me, Misty, how does it feel to be the person who will be flipping the switch to the new lighthouse?"

He shoved the microphone in her face.

"Uh," Misty muttered, staring blankly into the camera. "Um."

The reporter tried to help her out. "Are you thrilled?" he asked. "Excited? Tell everyone what it feels like!"

He tilted the microphone toward her.

"Yeah, well, uh . . . yeah."

The reporter looked at the camera and laughed. "Obviously, Miss Gordon is speechless! She's flipping out about flipping the switch! Reporting for ATVE, I'm Tom Blotswell!"

He rolled his eyes at Misty, then trotted off with his cameraman.

"Wow, Misty," said Yoshi, faking a look of awe. "You were sooooo interesting!"

"I thought you did just fine," said Mrs. Sweethouse, who had been watching. She handed Misty and Yoshi each a cup of hot cocoa. "Good luck tonight!" she called as the girls ambled off.

Misty and Yoshi could see the belly of Sam Port sticking out of the doorway of the Hum Rum Tavern. He was calling to everyone who passed.

"Cold?" he was saying to a tourist. "Then step inside Hum Rum Tavern and warm yer bones with some spiced wine!"

Mr. Port spotted Misty and Yoshi.

"Good afternoon," he said. "Here to see Mr. Yates?"

"Yes," said Misty, looking in the Dearly Departed's window, where she expected to see a sleeping Mr. Yates. Only, he wasn't there. In fact, neither was the couch he usually slept on.

"Mr. Yates has been busy all day," said Mr. Port. "He just sold that old couch right out of the window. Yep, he's been busy all right!"

"Busy?" said Misty in disbelief.

This, she had to see.

Mr. Port hadn't been kidding. Mr. Yates was in the middle of yet another transaction, shaking hands with a well-dressed couple and saying, "Thank you! And do come again to the Dearly Departed! People die all the time, so please do come again!"

Packages in hand, the customers brushed past Misty and Yoshi, while Mr. Yates plopped into a chair, obviously exhausted from the unexpected day's business.

"Hello there, young Gordon!" Mr. Yates called, waving them over. "Have a sit. Whew! Is that hot cocoa? Oh, please, may I have a sip?"

"Sure," said Misty, handing him her cup. She noticed that Mr. Yates looked very pensive. "Are you feeling all right, Mr. Yates?"

"Oh yes," he said. "I'm just a little restless, that's all." He scratched his chin. "I've got a strange feeling . . . the sort of feeling you get when you're expecting company."

"*Company*?" said Misty, her eyes narrowing. "What *sort* of company?"

"The company of . . . family," Mr. Yates said wistfully. "Which of course, is impossible . . . considering that all my family is dead. But still, I've got this most peculiar feeling, and I can't seem to shake it." He shrugged his shoulders. "It probably has something to do with the holidays."

Mr. Yates turned to the girls. "Well, anyhow, what brings you girls to the store?"

"We wanted to invite you to the lighting ceremony," said Misty.

"Ah, the lighting ceremony," said Mr. Yates. "I overheard some customers talking about it. Thank you for the invitation, but I think I'll stay here."

Just then, the pager beeped in Misty's pocket.

"Well, it's time for me to get going," she said. "Good-bye, Mr. Yates."

With a tinkling of bells, the girls left the Dearly Departed and returned to the crowded beach, where night had fallen. Here and there bonfires burned, around which people sat roasting wieners and marshmallows as they waited for the ceremony to begin.

"I'm off to the lighthouse," Misty announced to her family.

"I'll wait for you here," said Yoshi. "Good luck!"

Misty set off across the beach to the lighthouse. A few minutes later, she was at the door of the tall building. A technician greeted her and then escorted her through the doors and onto the elevator. Misty braced herself as they shot into the air and came to another stomach-lurching halt at the top.

The doors *whooshed* open.

"Right on time!" Dr. Figg cried, taking Misty by the hand and leading her to the huge curved window. As far as the eye could see, the beach twinkled with bonfires. The sky was a deep, dark blue, and the waves below glittered with starlight.

Dr. Figg pressed a button on the wall, and a panel dropped away from the window. He and Misty stepped out onto a balcony, into the brisk night air.

"See that switch?" said Dr. Figg, pointing to a silver lever at Misty's side. "That's the one you're going to flip. Are you ready?"

"I'm ready," said Misty.

"Good evening!" Dr. Figg called into a microphone.

Applause and whistles rose from the crowd, far below.

"It's an historic evening, indeed!" Dr. Figg cheered, his voice echoing down the beach. "In just seconds, Ashcrumb's new and revolutionary lighthouse will be turned on for the first time! Our guest of honor, Misty Gordon, will be flipping the switch. Let the countdown begin! Ten . . . nine . . . eight . . ."

The crowd picked up the countdown, thousands of voices calling out together, "seven . . . six . . . five . . . four . . ."

Misty's hand trembled excitedly above the switch.

". . . three . . . two . . . one!"

Misty flipped the switch. With a loud humming sound, the lighthouse's massive lantern was set in motion. On came the bright beacon of the superbeam.

Oohs and *ahs* rose from the crowd as the lantern rotated quickly, sending swaths of silvery light to the farthest reaches of the dark sky.

"Well done!" said Dr. Figg, walking Misty back inside. "That was splendid, truly splendid—"

SALLIE the computer interrupted him. "Dr. Figg," said the electronic voice inside the chamber. "There is a USO in question."

"What's a USO?" asked Misty.

"Unidentified Sailing Object," answered Dr. Figg seriously, observing a pale blip on the control panel screen. Then he ordered: "SALLIE, give me a scan."

Instantly, the lighthouse's beam halted its rotation, centered on a point upon the horizon, and sent out jets of light. More cheers and whistles rose from the crowd outside, who thought this was part of the show.

"Scan complete," said the computer. "It is an inbound ship.

Estimated time of arrival in Ashcrumb is approximately fifteen hours.

"How many passengers are aboard?" asked Dr. Figg, staring at the panel.

There was a pause, and then the computer answered, "Zero."

"*Zero*?" said Dr. Figg, puzzled. "There are *no* passengers?"

"That is affirmative," said SALLIE.

Dr. Figg's face turned white. He began to tap his fingers anxiously upon the panel. "SALLIE," he said, his voice now strained, "give me an enhanced scan. See if you can read the name of this USO."

At this, a pale purple light lasered from the tower and pulsed rapidly into the dark.

"Scan complete," said the computer. "Name of ship is *Royal Ashcrumb*."

Everyone in the room gasped. Misty's heart quickened.

"I was afraid this was going to happen," Dr. Figg said in a low voice.

"You were?" gulped Misty. "What do you mean?"

Dr. Figg shouted madly, "THIS COMPUTER IS ALREADY MALFUNCTIONING!" He pulled at his hair. "Not only does SALLIE think that a sunken ship is now sailing, she thinks it's doing so without a crew!" He spun around and pointed at some technicians. "Figure out what's going on. NOW!"

Like drones in a beehive, the men in lab coats began checking knobs and pushing buttons.

Dr. Figg smoothed his hair and turned to Misty.

"Misty," he said, "I apologize for this technical glitch. I'm afraid you must leave now so that we can assess the situation." Then he dropped his voice to a whisper, as if he didn't want the computer to hear him. "I'm afraid that SALLIE may have blown a fuse."

Misty nodded and headed to the elevator.

"Oh, and Misty," Dr. Figg added, weakly. "There's no sense in telling anyone about this . . . error. So would you mind keeping this to yourself?"

"My lips are sealed," promised Misty. Down the elevator shot. The doors whisked open and Misty scrambled to her family.

"What a show!" sang Misty's parents.

"Thanks," said Misty, trying to put on a smile. Then she pulled Yoshi away from the group.

"The computer detected the *Royal Ashcrumb*," Misty whispered.

"No way," said Yoshi. "Did it say when it might be here?"

"Tomorrow morning, around nine o'clock."

"It's really happening," said Yoshi. "What are we going to do?"

"I don't know," replied Misty.

The girls gazed out at the sea. It was hard to imagine that upon its calm, glistening waters, something dreadful was sailing toward them.

15

Unexpected Guests

Yoshi spent the night at Misty's house, but the girls didn't sleep a wink. All night long, they sat on the floor of Misty's room, trying to figure out Madame Zaster's riddle.

"The Golden Three were moved from Ashcrumb sand, and now they lie in the palm of your hand," Misty kept whispering, staring intently at the dark lines and golden marks in her hand.

Yoshi got up and looked out the window. "Oh no," she said. "The sun is rising." She looked frantically at Misty. "Time has run out to find the statues!"

"Don't give up just yet," said Misty. "Let's check the map and see where the ship is now."

They took out Captain Yates's sea chart and unfurled it. It was as they feared. The tiny ship had finished its journey across the Atlantic and was nearing the bay.

"We need a closer view of the bay," said Misty, putting the sea chart aside and unrolling the map of the colony of Ashcrumb, which depicted the ship still miles from landfall.

"Whew," said Yoshi with relief. "SALLIE's estimation was correct. It looks like we have at least a few hours before the *Royal Ashcrumb* comes ashore." She glanced at Misty. "What do you think?"

Misty scanned the map and grinned. "I'll tell you what I think," she said. "I *think* I just figured something out!"

Misty laid her marked hand—palm up—next to the map.

"I can't believe it," said Yoshi with a gasp. "The black lines in your hand are just like the roads on the map!"

Misty traced the line that ran along the bottom of her palm and matched it to the map. "This is Plunder Street," she said. "And this line . . . ," she said, tracing a second line that ran up the middle of her palm, "is Anchor Street. And this one," she gathered, tracing the third line that went across the top of her palm, "is Shadow Street."

Misty took a deep breath. "The golden marks must represent the location of the Golden Three! And if I'm guessing correctly, then that means that they are buried at the end of Shadow Street."

"What's at the end of Shadow Street?" asked Yoshi.

"Madame Zaster's house," said Misty. "We've got to get there quickly, so we'll have to take the Vespa."

Misty stuffed the scrolls into her bag, alongside Madame Zaster's glasses. "Let's get out of here before my family wakes up," she said, slinging her bag over her shoulder and motioning for Yoshi to follow her.

The girls scurried to the garage. "We're gonna need this thing," said Misty, grabbing the metal detector. Then the girls quickly pushed the Vespa down the driveway and hopped aboard. With the metal detector lying across its handlebars, Misty cranked on the scooter.

"Hang on tight!" Misty told Yoshi over her shoulder. "You know how rough the Vespa can be!"

Off they went.

Misty winded out the Vespa, whizzing down streets and cutting through yards until finally reaching the vine-covered sign marked SHADOW STREET.

"Get ready for the tree tunnel," said Misty. Cautiously, the girls rumbled down the dark street. The bare, gnarled limbs of the trees snatched at the girls' hair as they passed beneath them.

"How much farther?" Yoshi wailed.

"Just a little more," said Misty, her heart thumping.

Madame Zaster's house finally appeared.

"We're here," said Misty, halting the scooter and getting off, with the metal detector in hand.

"The statues are buried somewhere around this house," said Misty as she turned on the metal detector. Frantically, she began passing the detector over the yard, shooing some curious cats out of her way. "Come on!" she cried desperately, shaking the detector, which was only making static noises.

She moved closer to the porch, and suddenly the detector signaled a loud *WHOOP!*

"There's something here," Misty said.

Yoshi rushed over.

The girls dropped to their knees and began clearing the ground of slushy leaves.

Misty sighed. "It's a false alarm. It's just the path to Madame Zaster's house." She leaned over and cleared away more leaves from the path, revealing some round stones among the crushed shells. "I saw these stones the first time I was here with my dad."

Yoshi cocked her head. "But look!" she said. "There are exactly *three* of them!"

"Three?" squealed Misty. "Let's get to digging!"

Using their hands, the girls dug in the ground, which was soft with snowmelt. They worked on the first stone, moving around its edges, going deeper and deeper into the soil until they'd dug at least a foot deep.

"Get on the other side," said Misty, "and help me lift it out."

They grabbed the stone and pulled. Slowly, the object emerged, and then it popped out all at once.

"Wow," said Misty, her hair standing on end as she gazed upon the statue of Poseidon. Barely twelve inches tall, with a five-inch circular base, the slender golden statue, though covered in dirt, gave off a dazzling glimmer and felt warm to the touch. The girls excitedly brushed the dirt from his trident.

"Madame Zaster buried them upside down," said Yoshi, "so they'd look like small stepping-stones. How clever!"

They set Poseidon down and began digging up another statue.

With a few tugs, the girls extracted the statue of Zeus, poised with thunderbolt in hand.

A few minutes later, they had unearthed the statue of Hades. Unlike the other statues, Hades was not warm. He was cold and clammy. A feeling of dread overcame Misty as she picked up the golden god of the underworld and put him in her bag along with the other statues.

Misty slung the bag across her body, and the girls hopped onto the Vespa and took off.

"Now what are we going to do?" Yoshi cried as they sped back through the tree tunnel.

"You'll see!" said Misty. "Once we get to the beach, you'll see!"

They arrived at the seashore to find a crowd of people gathered at the base of the new lighthouse, staring out to sea as SALLIE's superbeam swirled through a thick fog that was rolling in.

A blast from the lighthouse's foghorn sounded, followed by SALLIE's computerized voice: "WARNING! UNMANNED SHIP APPROACHING BAY!"

Screams erupted from the crowd as the dark bow of a ship cut through the fog like a blade through white silk, her sails fluttering as the vessel splashed toward shore.

Through the shrieks and shouts, Misty could hear Mr. Lane yelping wildly in disbelief, "It's the *Royal Ashcrumb*!" followed by Sam Port hollering, "And she's a runaway! Sure enough— there's no one aboard! Batten down the hatch! She's a-comin'!"

Misty motored the scooter to the end of the peninsula and stopped. To the girls' relief, the craggy point was empty, save for a seagull poking about some seaweed.

They jumped off the Vespa, and Misty pulled the statue of Poseidon from her bag.

Misty stood for a moment, gathering her courage. Then she raised the statue of Poseidon in the air, aimed his trident toward the ocean, and commanded, "Poseidon, pass your power through me!"

From the points of the trident, three thin white streaks of

lightning shot. With a crackling noise, one streak arched into the sky like an electrified kite string, while the other two bright currents bowed into the ocean.

And then it began.

From the east there came a gust of wind so powerful that it blew Misty and Yoshi to their knees and sent the seagull somersaulting into the dunes. And then, as if night were falling in fast-forward motion, a wave of black clouds began to roll in, tumbling into themselves as they spread across the sky. No sooner had the clouds consumed the sky did the ocean begin to boil with dark and angry waves.

The statue was growing extremely hot, so Misty jammed it into the sand.

"Get down!" she called to Yoshi over the loud gales.

The girls both dropped to their stomachs and watched, awestruck, as the streaks from the trident continued to work their magic on the sky and sea. With an earsplitting clap of thunder, rain began falling in sheets. Straining against the wind and rain, Misty pulled Madame Zaster's glasses from her bag. She tossed her new glasses aside and put on Madame Zaster's. She looked out upon the sea.

Through the storm crashed the *Royal Ashcrumb*, pitched on her side, her sails shredding in the wind. While her ghost crew scrambled frantically about the deck, the leader of the Black

Adders stood fast at his post, with a sinister and determined look on his face.

To Misty's horror, the vessel was sailing closer—despite the screaming wind, despite the bitter rain, and despite the violent waves pouring overboard.

Her heart rising in her throat, Misty began to shake all over. She'd done all she could to stop the *Royal Ashcrumb*, and it hadn't been enough. "They're still coming," she said in shock. "They're still coming, they're still—"

At that moment, the entire sky went white, as if a flashbulb had gone off in the heavens. Then down shot a bolt of lightning, blowing Misty and Yoshi into the air. They landed in a spray of sand and blinked, stunned from the blast and even more stunned to see that the bolt of lightning that had fallen from the sky was *still* falling, its brilliant path into the ocean pulsating with fury.

The girls ducked as the mast of the ship exploded, catching the sails ablaze.

"Sink, sink, sink!" the girls chanted together.

With another gust of wind, the fiery ship was tossed completely on her side, allowing the churning waters to overtake her. Through the smoke and fire Misty could see the ghosts of the Black Adders splashing in the waves, while their captain held desperately to the mermaid upon the doomed ship's prow.

And with a giant wave, the ship and her ghost crew were gone, leaving nothing except a few black bubbles and a cloud of smoke that quickly turned to fog.

"We did it!" Misty cried, jumping up. "We did it!"

The girls gave a joyful scream, hopping up and down in the cold rain, while shouts of disbelief came from the crowd down the beach.

"Wow," said Misty. "Listen to them. They're going nuts!"

"And I'm going numb!" said Yoshi, her teeth chattering. "I'm freezing! Let's go home."

Misty nodded and picked up the hot statue of Poseidon and dropped it into her bag. "Oh no," she groaned, leaning over and feeling around in the sand. "I lost my new glasses!"

"We'll look for them later," said Yoshi.

The drenched girls stumbled through the sand and climbed back on the scooter, weary and shaking. Having taken a beating in the wild weather, the Vespa barely cranked on. Sputtering, it carried the girls roughly over the dunes, the statues clanking in Misty's bag with every bump in the beach.

The girls didn't say a word as they traveled past the lighthouse, where complete chaos had broken out over the unbelievable spectacle. Misty and Yoshi just kept their tired heads down as the Vespa weaved through the crowd of shocked onlookers, police officers, and TV crews.

Finally, Misty pulled in front of the Yamamoto's house.

Yoshi climbed off the scooter and smiled. "I still can't believe we did it!"

"I know," said Misty. "But we did! I'll call you later."

Yoshi smiled and waved.

Then Misty moved up the Gordons' driveway and parked the Vespa in the garage. With her bag in hand, she staggered inside her house to find her father waiting in front of the fire.

"There you are!" Mr. Gordon cried. "Where have you been? We've been worried about you."

He jabbed the fire with a poker, then sat down in his chair. "Your mother and James went to Plunder Street to look for you. They heard that there was something going on at the lighthouse and thought you might be there."

Still stunned from everything she'd just gone through, Misty didn't reply. She just stood quivering, her eyes big behind Madame Zaster's glasses.

"Sit down and warm up, Misty!" he said, pointing at the couch. "You're soaked to the bone."

Misty collapsed onto the couch, dropping her bag on the floor. It landed with a heavy clank.

"What on earth was that noise?" said Mr. Gordon, leaning

forward and giving the satchel a curious look. "What have you got in that old mailbag of yours?"

"It's a surprise," Misty grinned. "Open it and see."

"A surprise, ay?" he said. "Well, I love surprises."

He opened the bag and stuck a hand inside. Misty bit her lip as her father pulled out one of the statues. It was gleaming Poseidon, his trident still smoking.

Mr. Gordon stared at it, his eyes glittering. Spellbound, he moved it into the light of the fire, and the room filled with a soft golden glow.

"It's one of the Golden Three," he gasped. "You found the Golden Three!"

"Yes!" Misty cried, thrilled to see her father so happy. "Yoshi and I found them!"

"I don't believe it," he said as he pulled the statue of Zeus from the bag.

"What's more," said Misty, "I used the statue of Poseidon to sink the *Royal Ashcrumb*! The Black Adders are gone for good!"

But Mr. Gordon wasn't listening. He was feeling around in the bag.

"Where's the statue of Hades?" he said.

"It's in the bag," replied Misty.

"No, it's not," said Mr. Gordon.

"What do you mean?" said Misty, panicked. She threw open the bag and looked inside.

"Hades is gone!" she cried out in alarm.

"Think, Misty," said Mr. Gordon, holding her by the shoulders. "Where could it be? Try to remember!"

Misty shook her head, thinking. "I—I don't know," she stammered. "I was driving the Vespa . . . and it was riding pretty rough. The statue might have bumped out on the way here!"

There was a knock at the front door.

Mr. Gordon threw the statues of Poseidon and Zeus back into the bag and handed it to Misty. "Hide this!" he told her.

Misty dashed upstairs to her room and threw the bag in Madame Zaster's vanity.

She raced back to her father. Together they stood, stock-still, listening to the door creak open. Misty held her breath as she heard a shuffle of footsteps and a rattling noise.

"What the devil—" said Mr. Gordon, watching in horror as Hazel Monger and Fannie Belcher entered the room.

"It looks like you dropped some things on your way home, Misty Gordon," Fannie Belcher said darkly, pulling the statue of Hades and its scroll from a deep pocket of her fur coat. She waved them maliciously in the air and then shoved them back into her pocket.

Mr. Gordon pulled Misty to his side.

"D-d-do you see them?" Misty asked her father.

"Yes," he said gravely.

Misty's heart flopped. For if her father could see Hazel Monger and Fannie Belcher, it meant that the women were no longer dead.

"Where are the other statues?" snapped Hazel sharply.

Misty and Mr. Gordon didn't answer.

"You brat!" Belcher hissed at Misty. "Don't you see that the Descendants are back from the dead? Misty Gordon, I warned you not to interfere with the prophecy. Tell us where the other statues are right now . . . or else."

"Or else what?" said Mr. Gordon boldly.

From the shadows came a murky laugh. "Or else this . . ."

Into the firelight stepped the leader of the Black Adders. He grabbed Misty, while his two henchmen sprang from the gloom and held Mr. Gordon.

The pirate drew his sweaty face to Misty's ear and whispered, "Now, you be a good lass and fetch the other statues. 'Tis time the dream of the Snakes was realized. Soon we will rule the world! And nothing," he added, waving a blade in front of her face, "will stand in our way. Especially you, Misty Gordon."

"Take your hands off her!" yelled Mr. Gordon, trying to wrestle free from the clutches of the henchmen.

"As you wish," said the pirate, letting go of Misty and giving her a brutish shove. Misty fell to the floor, landing painfully on her knees.

"Get up!" Belcher screamed, stomping toward her.

Misty got unsteadily to her feet but then collapsed onto Belcher, her hands sinking into the sickening folds of musty mink.

"Take your hands off my coat, you clumsy little fool!" snapped Belcher, yanking Misty up by her hair. "Now, go get the other statues!"

"Do as they say, Misty," said Mr. Gordon.

Misty nodded to her father and then scurried to her room with her head down—and a smile on her face. For tucked under her sweater was the statue of Hades and its scroll that she had just deftly picked from Fannie Belcher's coat pocket.

Misty rushed to the vanity and took her bag from the drawer. She peeked into the bag at the shimmering statue of Zeus. "Please work," she whispered desperately.

"WE'RE WAITING, BRAT!" Hazel Monger's shrill voice traveled up the stairs.

Misty reappeared by the fireplace and stood still and quiet with her bag in hand.

"Well?" snarled Fannie Belcher, jerking her head. "Do you have them? Do you have the other statues?"

"Yes," said Misty.

"Then give them to us!" ordered the leader of the Black Adders, his eyes flickering red. "GIVE THE SNAKES WHAT THEY DESERVE!"

"*As you wish*," said Misty. She plunged her hand into the bag, pulled out the statue of Zeus, and cried, "Zeus, pass your power through me!"

At that moment, an ominous hum sounded from above, as if a giant wheel was spinning upstairs.

"What *is* that?" snapped Hazel Monger, staring at the ceiling, which had begun to glow. Then the entire house began to vibrate, sending furniture rumbling along the floor and rattling windows. As the humming grew louder, the fireplace began to pulse, as if it were breathing flames.

All of a sudden, a shaft of golden light shot down the chimney and lit on Zeus's thunderbolt, sending it spinning like a propeller, faster and faster until it was a gleaming blur. Then, to Misty's astonishment, the very arm of Zeus began to move, drawing back and taking aim with his thunderbolt.

Realizing the statue was setting its sight on them, Fannie Belcher and Hazel Monger fled. Cursing and shrieking, they tripped over one another on their way to the door. But they did not make it.

The statue hurled its golden bolt toward Fannie and Hazel. Like an arrow on fire, the bolt flew across the room, and with a deafening *ZING,* seared through both of them, simultaneously vaporizing Fannie Belcher and Hazel Monger in a shower of flickering light.

The Snakes flung Mr. Gordon aside and watched in dread as the gleaming statue of Zeus plucked another golden bolt from thin air and drew its aim upon them.

"Wait," Misty commanded the statue, when she saw the leader of the Snakes about to speak. The statue obeyed, holding back the crackling bolt while the leader stepped forward.

Misty watched suspiciously as the pirate slowly removed his black hat and gave her a patronizing bow. He straightened up and glared at Misty, his dark eyes narrow with disbelief. Then he gazed greedily at Zeus. "The Snakes had great plans," he said resentfully, his voice rising. "Plans of power and untold fortune." Then he turned his eyes back to Misty. "You could be a part of these plans, Misty Gordon."

He drew out her name as if he were hissing, leaving his mouth hanging open nastily. Then he took a step forward.

"Aye," he murmured, his chin raised defiantly. "You are just a child. You cannot possibly conceive of the true powers of the Golden Three. You don't have it in you." He gave a sickening smile. "But the Snakes can show you. That is . . . if you're willing to make a deal."

He took another step forward. He was so close now that

Misty could smell the odor of rot upon him. "Spare the Snakes," he said persuasively, an oily tone to his voice, "and we'll show you what amazing things you can achieve with the Golden Three."

Misty's eyes began to glaze. She felt as if something was snuffing out her heart and twisting her mind. Her grasp upon the statue began to weaken as she realized that what the pirate was saying was true. How *could* an eleven-year-old girl even *begin* to understand what the Golden Three could do? Maybe she really *didn't* have it in her to conceive of the sheer greatness of it all.

"So," said the pirate, cocking his head to the side. "Do we have a deal?"

Misty paused as a bright golden light flickered from Zeus and lit the side of the pirate's neck, illuminating his tattoo— reminding Misty that he was nothing more than a Snake.

"Do we have a deal?" he repeated.

"NO!" shouted Misty.

The pirate's mouth curled up in rage, and he sprang toward the statue, only to be met with the golden thunderbolt through his neck. The pirate stumbled backward as he caught ablaze.

Out of the corner of her eye, Misty saw more bolts shoot from the statue. The roaring flames jetted through the flailing leader and both of his henchmen. Their flesh flashed bright gold and then went to bones. For a moment, their skeletons stood, black and charred, until disintegrating into heaps of ash on the floor.

Misty staggered as a howling, hot wind tore through the house, whirling the ashes into the air and back up the chimney. With a final flash, everything went quiet.

"They're gone," said Misty. "They're really gone!"

Mr. Gordon nodded and gave Misty a big hug. Then Misty placed the Golden Three upon the mantel. Together, Misty and her father stood back and gazed in awe upon the gleaming statues.

"Now that we have the Golden Three," asked Misty, "what are we going to do with them?"

"First things first," said Mr. Gordon. "And that's hide them. In fact, they need to be hidden right now. Your mother and brother will be returning soon."

Mr. Gordon slipped the statues into Misty's bag. "Here you go," he said, handing the bag to Misty. "Find a safe place for them while I clean up this mess."

For a moment, Misty stood with bag in hand while her father began putting their furniture back in place.

"Well," said Mr. Gordon, looking up, "what is it, Misty?"

"I—I—" Misty stammered, "I just thought *you* might want to hide the statues. I figured they're yours . . . since you've been looking for them all these years."

Mr. Gordon smiled and patted Misty on the head.

"Misty," he said, "the Golden Three belong to you. It's obvious that I wasn't meant to find them. *You* were."

A car could be heard pulling into the driveway.

"Sounds like they're home," said Mr. Gordon. "And unless you want James to control the world, you better hide those statues!"

"You're right!" Misty laughed, hurrying up to her room.

Luckily for Misty, she already had the perfect hiding place for the statues: Madame Zaster's vanity.

Misty placed the bag into one of the vanity's drawers. "You protected the scrolls," Misty whispered to the vanity, "and now you've got something even more important to guard."

As if accepting the task, the drawer shut on its own.

Just then, the palm of Misty's hand began to tingle. She looked, surprised to see the dark lines and golden marks quickly fading away. And just like that, they were gone.

16

The Beach

"Misty made the newspaper again!" Mr. Gordon announced Sunday morning at breakfast.

"I did?" said Misty, peering over his shoulder, and then reading the headline of the *Daily Ashcrumb*'s weekend edition aloud:

MISTY GORDON USHERS IN

A NEW LIGHT TO ASHCRUMB

Mrs. Gordon clapped her hands. "Oh, and look at Misty's picture!" she gushed, pointing to the photograph of Misty throwing the switch at the lighting ceremony. "You look so pretty in your new glasses!"

Even James had to agree. "Yeah," he grunted. "You don't look as grotesque as you did the last time your picture was in the paper."

"Thanks, James," said Misty, rolling her eyes behind the cat-eye glasses.

"Come to think of it," added James, plowing into some bacon, "why are you wearing those ugly glasses again?"

"I lost my new ones at the beach yesterday," replied Misty. "The wind blew them right off my head during the storm."

"That was the most wicked storm ever!" said James excitedly. "It drove that runaway ship right into the bay!"

"Well, according to the *Daily Ashcrumb*," noted Mrs. Gordon, "it wasn't a runaway ship but rather an old, unmanned fishing boat that had gotten loose in the foul weather."

"Fishing boat?" coughed Misty, dropping her toast.

"That's right," chirped Mrs. Gordon, referring to the paper. "That's what authorities surmised. They also say that the fog caused the rest of the confusion."

"*Rest of the confusion*?" said Misty.

"Evidently," explained Mrs. Gordon, "the murky mist fooled some witnesses into thinking they were seeing the *Royal Ashcrumb*!"

"Aw, man," said James disappointedly. "So it wasn't the *Royal Ashcrumb*, after all?"

"Of course not!" snorted Mrs. Gordon. "Don't be ridiculous."

"That's right, son," said Mr. Gordon as he gave a side-wink to Misty. "Don't be ridiculous."

⌒

After breakfast, Misty met Yoshi outside.

"Want to help me find my lost glasses at the beach?" said Misty.

"Sure," said Yoshi. "Let's go."

A sunny and beautiful morning, it was perfect weather for a walk. The two friends took their time on their way to the beach, allowing Misty the chance to fill Yoshi in on everything that had happened since they'd last seen each other.

"So the Golden Three are safe and sound," said Yoshi as they reached the dune where Misty had lost her glasses.

"Yes," said Misty as they spread out and searched the glistening sand. "They're safe and sound."

Suddenly, Misty jumped. "Here they are!" she cheered as she spotted her new glasses in a clump of seaweed. She picked them up and wiped the grit from them. "Oh good!" she added. "The lenses aren't broken. What a relief. I couldn't bear wearing Zaster's glasses one more minute!"

Just as Misty was reaching to remove the cat-eye glasses, they became icy cold and the lenses fogged over.

"Oh no," said Misty. "*Not again.*"

Yoshi called. "What do you see?"

"Madame Zaster," replied Misty as the ghost appeared to her.

"*I've come to bid you farewell, Misty Gordon,*" said the apparition, which was dressed in a cloak this time, as if it were going on a journey. "*And to congratulate you and Yoshi on a job well done. The Golden Three are safe . . . for now.*"

"*For now?*" said Misty. "What do you mean?"

"*Even though the Black Adders and two of their Descendants have been destroyed,*" the ghost explained, "*there will always be those who will try to get their hands on such powerful and magical treasure.*

"*Even now,*" continued the ghost, "*there are forces at work that will stop at nothing to find the statues.*"

"What forces?" asked Misty, exasperated.

"*You will learn in time,*" replied the ghost as it began to fade away.

"But what should I do with the Golden Three?" asked Misty desperately. "Why do I have them? For what purpose? Please tell me!"

"*You will learn in time, Misty Gordon,*" repeated the ghost, and with a light breeze, the apparition vanished from view.

"What just happened?" asked Yoshi, walking up. "I was too far away from you to hear Madame Zaster."

"I'll tell you all about it later," said Misty.

With that, Misty removed the cat-eye glasses and slipped on her new pair.

"So . . . ," wondered Yoshi, "now that you've got your new glasses back, what are you going to do with Madame Zaster's?"

"I think I'll keep them for now," said Misty, dropping them into her coat pocket. "*Just in case I need to see more than meets the eye.*"

"Good idea," laughed Yoshi. "Someone really smart must have given you that advice."

"Yeah," said Misty with a grin. "I wonder who!"

And the two friends turned and headed back home.

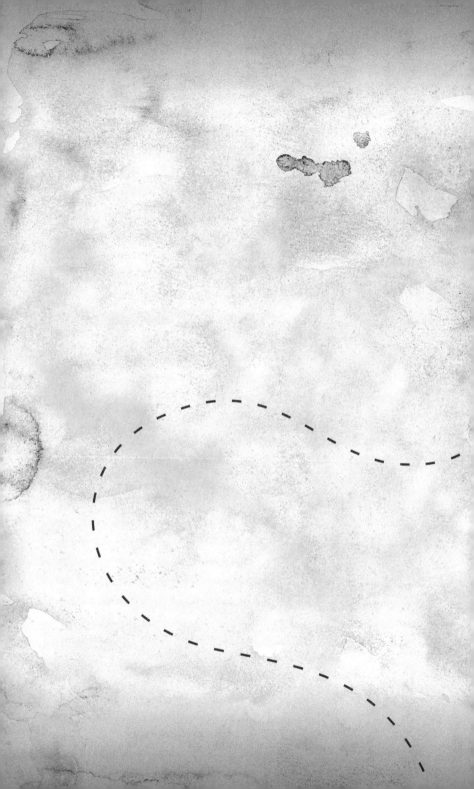

About the Author

Kim Kennedy has collaborated on a number of books with her brother Doug, including *Pirate Pete*, *Pirate Pete's Giant Adventure*, *Pirate Pete's Talk Like a Pirate*, and *Hee-Haw-Dini and the Great Zambini*. This is her first novel. She lives with her husband in Louisiana.

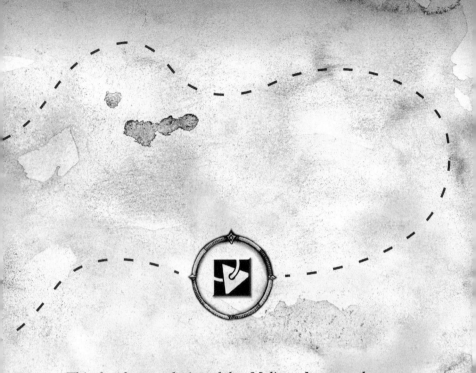

This book was designed by Melissa Arnst and art directed by Chad W. Beckerman. The main text is set in Wilke, which was designed by the famous Berlin font artist Martin Wilke and presented by Linotype AG in 1988. Wilke was influenced in part by the letters of the Irish handwriting in the Book of Kells, written in the late eighth century, while the pronounced contrast in strokes goes back to the eighteenth century.

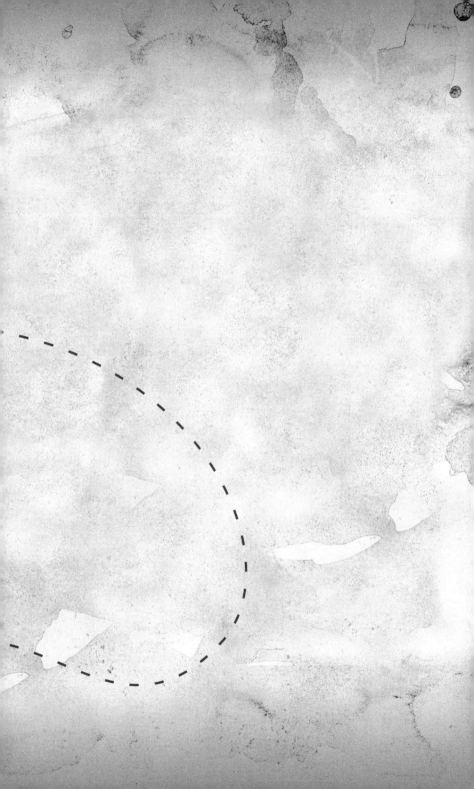

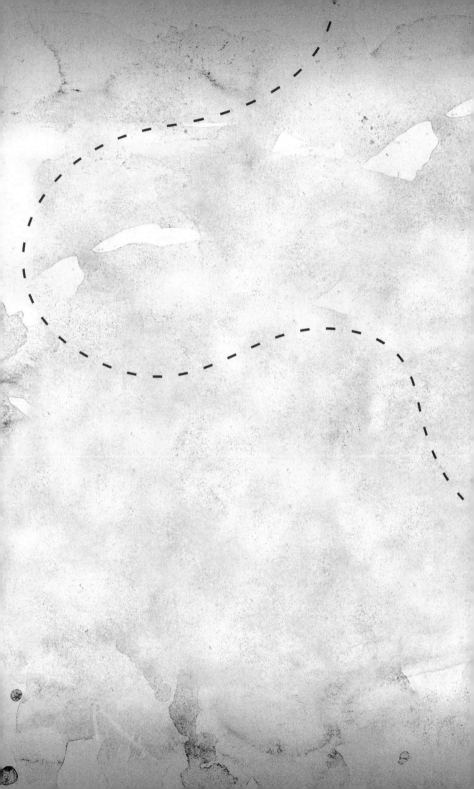

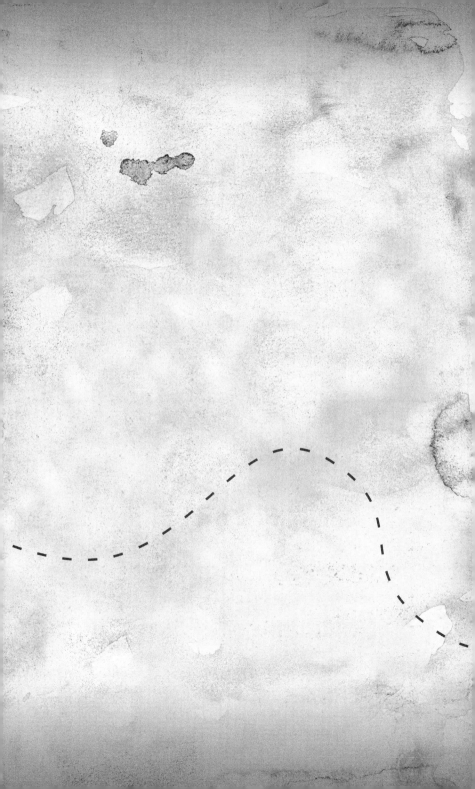